THE PARTING GIFT

ALSO BY EVAN FALLENBERG

When We Danced on Water

Light Fell

THE PARTING GIFT

EVAN FALLENBERG

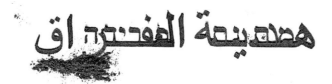

OTHER PRESS / NEW YORK

Copyright © 2018 Evan Fallenberg
Production editor: Yvonne E. Cárdenas
Text designer: Jennifer Daddio
This book was set in Horley Old Style MT and Centaur MT
by Alpha Design & Composition of Pittsfield, NH

1 3 5 7 9 10 8 6 4 2

LIBRARY OF CONGRESS CATALOGING-IN-PUBLICATION
DATA TK

FOR MICHA AND HAGAI,

boundlessly

Dear Adam,

We are sitting, as I write this, as we often do: me on the sofa and you at your desk, your back to me, hunched over your computer. Your hair needs cutting, this time preferably by someone—anyone—other than Beth. You will never see, as I can, the line, or lack of one, that runs from below your left ear to below your right, how jagged it is, how unendearing. Your nape—what a lovely, raw word, don't you think? So Saxon and blunt—is impossibly white, sickly white, and the mole that is nearly equidistant between your scraggly hairline, such as it is, and the collar of your stretch-necked T-shirt, stands out like a nipple on a pale breast. A nipple on a pale breast: a beautiful metaphor, wouldn't you agree? It retains the bodily imagery but swivels it around from front to back. I hope you don't feel it emasculates you, though. Beth wouldn't approve, she's a fierce defender of your masculinity. Such as it is. The lady doth protest a little too much.

Your nape, still bent to your work, still deathly white with a dark eruption that contains who knows what disease or tumor one day to awaken and poison you, invites kissing or strangling. I could do either, in fact. Now, though, I'm too distracted for either. I'm occupied, gainfully, with this letter, which is, or will be, my parting gift to you. In it I shall recount how it is that I washed up on your doorstep nearly four months ago, and what events brought me here. You have never asked me and I find that exceedingly nice of you—
nice being a word that could have been coined specially for you had it not already been abused for centuries in describing the bland or the sweet or the cuddly or the mild—and at the same time exceedingly odd. Would I ever do the same for you, or anyone? Doubtful. But you,

Adam, you are not me and I am not you, so it is a good thing that I was the one who did the washing up on the doorstep and you who did the welcoming.

I should stand up from the sofa and pull your shoulders back to keep you from slouching so terribly. You do it all the time, and recently, even when you stand to your full medium height, you do it; you are slowly slipping into the form of a question mark, when at your age you should be an exclamation mark, erect and definitive. I have spoken to you about this, in a friendly way of course, and on one memorable occasion—I know you remember it, Adam, maybe more than you'd like?—I bent down to you from behind, lassoed one arm around your neck and straightened your head against my abs. Your fingers hovered over your keyboard. It was so awkward for you! You didn't know whether you should just carry on tapping as if I weren't holding you, as if we weren't breathing in sync, or whether you should give in and let me move your body as it should be moved. Beth, I'd guess, doesn't do that for you, does she? No, you're the man and you do the moving, the placing, the laying on of hands. Of course you do.

But I still haven't properly explained why I'm writing this letter to you when you are a matter of two paces across the room from me and unable to keep from hearing any words I might let slip from between my lips. You are my captive audience, and too polite to ignore me no matter how much I am getting on your nerves after one hundred and eleven days on the sofa in your tiny apartment (I've counted). Oh, I know I'm getting on your nerves, testing your resolve to be generous and undemanding, to practice what you preach about a kinder, gentler world in which we look after one another instead of solely our selves. You loathe hoarding and selfishness and greed. How right you are that we are destroying all that is good around us, from natural resources to human relationships, and you are out there doing something about

it, making a difference, making of yourself
and your Project a shining example. And
along I've come and plopped myself down in
the middle of all that like some man-made
eyesore—I'm thinking of a dam on a pristine
river, strip-mining in a jungle; our old lit-theory
prof would be proud of my "consistency of
metaphor," don't you think?—which you are
dealing with so admirably, so fairly, with such
generosity of spirit. Beth has told you to get rid
of me, I know it, I see it on her face daily; your
mother has too, judging by a phone conversation
I overheard last week. But you, Adam, you have
stood your ground for one hundred and eleven
days and I imagine you could hold out for one
hundred and eleven more—a thousand and
eleven, why not?!—but I will spare you that, I
will save you the rift with your girlfriend and
your mother and your conscience and in this
case it will be me who does the decent thing,
the selfless thing; and that is the purpose of this
letter, my friend: I am leaving, in fact I shall

be gone when you are reading this. It will be the long-overdue explanation of my mysterious appearance at your door these four months ago. The expression of my gratitude.

I expect you will be tempted to share this letter with Beth, your beloved, from whom you have surely pledged to hide nothing. But my recommendation is that you read it through first in secret, alone; if nonetheless you decide to let her read it then at least it will be a decision made from knowledge and not from some promise you made about open communication, or from guilt. I detest guilt as a motivating factor for anything, and as for the promises made between lovers, well, they are a blueprint for calamity, a writ of divorce rendered point by point. You'll think I'm being cynical here—you've used that word on me on five occasions in these four months already— but I have more experience in this than you do. Beth, you feel certain, would break no vows made or even implied between you, and you have had no true lover before Beth, so she is the entirety of your experience, and you two as a couple are untried. But take it from me, a man with a record in the crimes of love: Promises will be broken and vows will be trampled and feelings will be hurt—oh, far worse than that. Where love is concerned the rules are not written in books of statutes but they exist all the same, and they are unbending.

But I don't wish to turn you away—not from Beth, not from love, and not from me and the story I am about to reveal to you in these pages. So do not worry your sweet head about it, that head of unwashed, uncoiffed hair, or for that matter your gently sloping back or your hairless arms and legs or your hollow belly or sweet, bony ass. Carry on with your Project—you are typing now, furiously; it looks, from the sofa, to be yet another grant application, another long Statement of Purpose or Scope of Project essay—and do not let me distract you unduly. But do read my recounting, my accounting, and let it penetrate you at the margins of the day, when you lie in bed, your arm curled gently around a soporific Beth; let it infiltrate your pores, allow it to seep in to your soul. You are too pure, my friend; perhaps this will be your chance for damnation.

This story, like most stories, could begin in a number of different places. I could slip backward in time all the way to my grandparents in order to show you what kind of households my parents grew up in. I could start when you and I met, in grad school, so that the arc of this narrative would become our story, the story of our acquaintanceship. There are other options, and literary techniques we learned together and could both name, that would do the trick as well, but I'll spare you the gimmickry and cut to the facts that hounded me all the way to this living room on 119 Maple Street in this wannabe bohemian neighborhood of this middling city of America. For the record, I will tell this story with the utmost objectivity I can muster, an attempt at The Truth. I urge you to read without skepticism, but since you are generally guileless and gullible I believe you will believe what I report to you, as you should. To make this accounting as readable as possible I will write it not so much as a letter, not so much as a recounting through my eyes, but as reportage, which means that I will give you the scenes as they happened, and with dialogue between the various characters that is as authentic as I can recall—and authentic it will be, since my memory is phenomenal and photographic, or whatever the audio equivalent is called. Surely you remember how I could imitate our profs, reciting whole monologues of theirs even days after hearing them, so it should come as no surprise that these events I am about to share, these events of great portent and drama that caused a grand detour in my life, should be etched onto my consciousness in such a way that they are accessible to me in bulk.

Beyond the story itself, Adam, I think you'll simply enjoy reading this because it will be well written even without editing; time is short, revisions take long, and my writing is strong enough to present you with a first draft. I know what a good reader you are and you know what a fine vocabulary I have, my way with a sentence. Even in a graduate program in literature I stood out, right? So you can be guaranteed that I will deliver you a work of elegance and original insight.

So, Adam, leave your computer, lay aside your Project, come sit upon this very sofa, recently vacated. Turn on the reading lamp, pour yourself a cup of that awful instant coffee you drink incessantly, pull the afghan over your legs if it's as cold in here as it is today, and read me for a few hours. As in life, I will never bore you.

You remember, I'm sure, that I left our grad program under highly unpleasant circumstances a few months shy of graduation. It was February at the time, bleak and bracing, and I needed to

get as far away as possible. So I went to Israel
for the warm weather and because my Hebrew
is passable—you know that my mother's Israeli,
right? I don't discuss it much, but there's no
denying her accent; if you met her you would
know in an instant. She over-enunciates; she
tries to move her *r*'s forward from her throat but
overdoes it and they get thrust to the front and
come out as *w*'s; she stretches short vowels into
long ones. She fancies herself an L.A. matron
but she'll always be a foreigner, with a foreign
accent and foreign friends. My mother can't
stand her parents so we didn't go there much,
but I heard enough Hebrew in my childhood
to understand pretty well and I figured I could
get myself around the country without too
much difficulty, so I bought a one-way ticket to
Tel Aviv and showed up there without telling
anyone I was coming.

I also chose Israel because if you're a Jew
you can get off the plane in Tel Aviv, tell them
you want to be a citizen, and you get processed

right there at the airport. Full rights and benefits—housing, education, medical. The works. I mean, how desperate can a country be? That's fucked up. Of course, you really have to be Jewish, but it was no problem proving that, thanks to my mom. For once it felt like she was helping me out instead of standing in my way.

So, I got a place to stay at an absorption center for new immigrants. In the middle of Tel Aviv, no less, where rentals are nearly as expensive as New York and as hard to come by. It was only good for a few months, but I figured I would have something worked out for myself by the time I had to move out. June I sounded like it was years off in the future.

Once I got settled I called my mother's brother, but he was a prick and told me it wasn't a good time for me to come visit. I swear he was making up an excuse as we spoke. I never phoned him again the whole time I was in the country and I was beginning to believe that all that ranting my mother did over the years about her family was probably true. I didn't even bother with my grandparents at all. I hadn't seen them for about fifteen years, since my bar mitzvah, where they behaved like primitives. My grandmother started ululating—it's that tongue-wagging call they make in Arab countries that sounds like turkeys in the wild— and my grandfather kept trying to sell some bogus piece of desert land he owns to my dad's rich Angelino friends. My mom actually had to shove them in a taxi and send them to their hotel in the middle of the party. I don't think we even saw them again before their flight home. So anyway, there was no point in letting them know I was in Israel.

Those first few months weren't bad at all. I dumbed down my Hebrew so I'd be able to study in an *ulpan*, a kind of language school, which is where my social life took place, too. I went to all the cool stuff happening in Tel Aviv all the time—parties, gallery openings, film festivals, art festivals, food festivals; the nightlife starts at eight or ten or midnight and never really ends. I got out to the bars and the beaches, too. I brought men home, sometimes women with them, too. It was really easy to pick people up and get picked up. My looks have always drawn people to me—you must remember that from school, how even the teachers wanted a piece of me—but this was a little insane. You'd think the country was lacking in tall, slim guys with a five o'clock shadow and Ray-Bans. Funny, they always knew I was American by my clothes, I guess, or other things: one dude told me my teeth looked American. And that all made me even more desirable, more attractive to them. I was getting it every day, twice a day if I wanted, and with great-looking people.

But all this is just background, my friend, for the true story, which begins in May, a couple of months after I'd landed in Tel Aviv and just about two weeks before I had to find a new place to live. Friends of mine from the ulpan were driving north with an Israeli friend who owned a car, and they invited me to come with them for the weekend, which runs from Thursday night to Saturday night. The plan was to camp out on a beach on the Sea of Galilee and make little day trips in the area. We had St. Peter's fish in Tiberias and saw a wooden boat from the time of Jesus that had been dredged from the sea. We did a little mild bed-jumping but nothing remarkable. On Saturday we packed it in early because Ariella, the Israeli girl with the car, had to get back to Tel Aviv for a family event.

"I will be boring," she told us. She was always doing that, getting her descriptive adjectives crossed. She had already called herself depressing and exciting and I was getting used to it.

"Bored," Maya corrected her. "You'll be bored." Maya was from Buenos Aires. Her English was great and her Hebrew wasn't bad, either. Her boyfriend, Danny, was also in class with us. I'd thought about seducing him in Tiberias but Maya made this lamb stew to die for and I didn't want to lose her friendship. He was sitting in back with me.

We'd crossed the Galilee and had just turned onto the highway that runs south along the Mediterranean coast and ends in Tel Aviv, when Maya repositioned herself to look at Ariella in the driver's seat. I got her face—the sharply sloping nose, the frame of brown, wavy hair in perfect profile. "Ariella," she said, "since we've still got time, why don't we stop at the Spice Guy on the way home. The article said he's open on Saturdays."

They had been talking about it on and off all weekend. The Spice Guy, as they called him, was someone they'd read about in a lifestyle magazine who specialized in the herbs and spices of the region and supposedly had the biggest variety and freshest wares around. A few of the trendier restaurants in Tel Aviv bought from him, as did some important Israeli clients abroad.

Ariella glanced at the clock on the dashboard. "Okay, but only for a little while."

A little while. I remembered that in the coming weeks and months and laughed about it.

We crossed a patch of highway so close to the sea that white sand threatened to spill onto the road with the slightest wind, and we veered off the interchange and onto a local road that led into a tiny town on a cliff over the beach. Maya navigated us easily with a few rights and lefts until we pulled up at a clump of several low buildings one block from the sea. When we got out of the car we stretched and took in the salty air.

In L.A., property one block off the beach would be huge and landscaped to perfection. But this was Israel: some of the buildings on this parcel of land were pretty decrepit, the garden was neglected and there was old farm equipment strewn all over the place. "Are you sure this is it?" Danny asked. No one answered.

I led the way in. The little house on the corner of the property was clearly not the spice center, so we walked to the left and entered what I would later learn was a converted chicken coop that, in its day, provided a panoramic million-dollar view of the sea to its feathered occupants. Now it was a covered market in two long rows with a center aisle, and as we sauntered slowly down it we caught the scent—a fresh, green smell of earth and produce—and read the signs, which gave the Hebrew and Latin names of everything. We meandered through the section offering dozens of kinds of mushrooms, from familiar oyster mushrooms and champignons and shiitake to shimeji, which looked like they'd been plucked from the bottom of the ocean, and pink oysters and golden trumpets, colorful fungi that were beautiful and utterly unappetizing. They came from farms and villages around Israel, places we did not know and could scarcely envisage.

The next section of the former coop was devoted to organic vegetables, most of which looked familiar but especially healthy and fresh. A few, like the Jerusalem artichoke or the round, deep-green zucchini, were new to me. Maya and Ariella were already loading up wire baskets they'd picked up at the entrance; Danny, bored without a screen in front of him, had moved quickly down the aisle and was out the other end. The three of us lingered, discussing the meals we would prepare with the succulent ingredients we were lifting, inspecting, and dropping into the baskets.

It took us probably twenty minutes to reach the spices and herbs at the end of the long, wide aisle. In all that time, no one bothered us or even appeared on the scene. I'd gone back for a third basket, so it was mine that began to fill up with bunches of cilantro and parsley and dill and spearmint. There were small clear plastic bags for holding the spices we were scooping up, and I chanted them to myself like a nursery rhyme: ginger, fennel seeds, cardamom, thyme. Cumin, oregano, cinnamon, sage. We sniffed them, took some to our tongues, read the little signs that offered suggestions about what to use them for.

"Check this out," Maya said. She was cupping a dark-yellow mound of powder. I stooped to smell it. "Cumin," she told me. "But I've never smelled it so...strong before."

I didn't know much about spices back then. Our home cuisine was American, not Middle Eastern in any way, and my mother was a big fan of Lowry's seasoning salt and used it on everything. Something about that cumin beckoned to me. I wanted to sniff it right up into my nose. For a very long minute I just stood there bent almost in half, my hands behind my back, the tip of my nose nearly touching the hillock of yellow cumin in Maya's palm. Finally she laughed and said, "Hey dude, I need my hand back. Get your own pile of cumin."

Ariella gave me some caraway seeds and sesame, which she called *kimmel* and *sumsum*, and we nibbled our way down the aisle. Maya called out to Danny, whom we could see outside the coop petting a dog. Up in Tiberias we had roasted under the sun, but here, late in the day and by the sea, there was a gentle breeze, and the coop was pleasant. I noticed several industrial-sized fans spread through the coop, but they were silent.

We talked some more, sniffed some more, filled our little baggies with spices we would probably never use, though Maya and Ariella couldn't stop planning meals as we went. Fish dishes, meats, salads. Middle Eastern, Indian, South American. I got caught up in their repartee and offered suggestions; with their excitement I knew I would be eating the results of this spree more than cooking them.

We had been there for nearly an hour when I went looking for someone to pay for all the goodies we'd gathered. The only soul I met was the dog Danny had been petting, a caramel-colored short-haired breed with a pointy nose like the kind you see on the tombs of the pharaohs. (Adam, you know from the fiasco with that yapping chow at Beth's sister's house that I'm no great fan of dogs, but I didn't cause it to tumble down the stairs on purpose no matter what she thought.) It was quiet and no one was about. I wandered around in the messy yard and finally entered a little building that clearly wasn't one of the houses on the property. I could see someone toward the far wall, his back to me and crouching so that only the baseball cap on his head was showing. I made my way toward him, past shelves crammed full with boxes and appliances and light fixtures and I don't even know what—just rows and rows of stuff that wouldn't pass muster at a yard sale. What I saw when I reached him was the upended lawn mower he was working on and his naked, slightly hairy back. The black waistband of his underwear rose above the belt on his olive-green work pants, which sported a few tools and a telephone pouch that seemed to be empty.

"We want to pay," I said in my blunt, unripened Hebrew.

"Okay," he told me, not looking up from the lawn mower. "In a minute." I was already accustomed to a sales style unlike here in the States, where salespeople pretend they're your best friend and sometimes tell you their whole pathetic life story when all you want is to buy a pair of jeans. Over there, in Israel, they act more like they couldn't give a fuck if you buy or not. I looked around again at the mess and was about to go back to my friends when he spoke up.

"It was the carburetor," he said. "One of my idiot employees used old gasoline from a rusty can." He popped a few screws into place, wiped his hands on an oil-black towel lying next to him and stood up, his back still to me. I could see that he was a few inches shorter than I but still a good six feet tall, and very broad. He

grabbed a T-shirt and as he turned to face me
he took off his hat and mopped the top of his
bald head. The hair under his arm was light,
almost blond, and I could smell him. Oh yes,
I could definitely smell him, and everything
that eventually happened may have started
at that particular moment, with the scent of
him rolling off in waves and wafting under
my untested nose. I've smelled you too, Adam,
your real true scent under that cloying body
spray you use to cover up any connection to
the real physical world, but yours is different:
it has no body, no weight to it. Your smell is
thin, gaseous, almost like legumes cooking on
a stovetop. This man standing in front of me,
though, his smell was meaty, truly pungent and
ripe. I was drawing it in through my nostrils
and holding it there, letting it shoot straight
into my limbic system, that ancient part of the
brain where memory and emotion and lust and
smell get entangled.

He was facing me now, still mopping himself but lower: his chest and armpits. I stood watching. His chest and belly were thick with honey-colored curly hair, his nipples large and erect. He was going about his business with no mind to me, while I was going about his business with no mind to myself. I didn't know then what it was that I found so riveting, but I clearly couldn't stop watching him touch himself. When he was done, he tossed the shirt over his head and his naked chest disappeared behind a faded green T-shirt with a logo I couldn't read.

"What did you want to buy?" he asked me.

"My friends. They're outside," I said, slightly breathless, pointing over my shoulder.

He brushed past me to lead the way out, his hand on my back to turn me to the right direction. I followed him out of the large shed, back to the yard and into the coop with the spices, where Maya and Ariella and Danny were chatting over the wire baskets and the dog was standing at attention.

"Are you Uzi?" Ariella asked him as he walked behind the counter, where there was a computer and a cash register I hadn't noticed before.

"Yeah."

"Uzi the Spice Guy," Maya added, almost to herself.

He looked at her but said nothing. My friends handed over the baskets and he weighed and punched in numbers until eventually he came up with a grand total that could have been a completely bogus number but I suspected was not. He dumped everything into plastic bags with the same logo as his T-shirt and handed them over.

Maya and Danny and Ariella took out their wallets and paid in cash.

"This is a really great place," Maya said to Uzi. "We read about you in *Haaretz*."

He nodded. He may have smiled but it was hard to tell under the sandy beard and mustache that covered the lower half of his face.

I stood watching all of them. My friends from Tel Aviv, this man, the Spice Guy. Uzi. I said nothing. I did not move. I wasn't even thinking, though I believe now that the powerful smell from his body may have been trapped in my nostrils and affecting my brain. Maya and Ariella and Danny pocketed their change; Danny lifted two of the bags, Maya and Ariella one each of the others. They said goodbye, thanked Uzi, started heading for the front of the coop. Uzi was busy with the cash register.

He'd pressed a button and the day's transactions were scrolling forth.

"Yoo hoo," Maya called back to me from the vegetable section. "What d'you forget?"

I stood there, immobile. "I'm staying," I called back.

Ariella and Danny stopped at the entrance. Uzi looked up from the register, as if noticing me for the first time. I looked him straight in the eye and said it again, softer this time, to him only. "I'm staying."

There must have been some fuss and bother. My friends must have asked questions, may even have come back to the spot at which I was rooted and touched me, pulled me even, but I have no recollection of any of that. I found my travel bag parked neatly by the entrance to the coop sometime later—that day, or the next or the next, when I started thinking about the real life of toothbrushes and fresh underwear. But what I do know is that within a matter of minutes they had driven off and I was still there, in that lousy coop, facing a man I did not know. He was leaning back against the wall now, studying me. He seemed amused, or curious, but only very slightly so, as if this sort of thing had happened before, or could happen within the realm of a day's activities: sort the incoming produce, tabulate the day's profits, process the guy who has decided to stay.

He leaned, his legs spread wide, his arms folded. I stood, my hands hanging straight at my sides. There was a counter between us, with a computer and a cash register and lots of scuff marks and gouges. The dog had disappeared, the sun was nearly down, the breeze had evaporated.

It seemed time for something to happen and I may have wondered why he didn't ask what I wanted, why I hadn't joined the friends I'd come with for the car ride back to Tel Aviv, but he merely leaned and looked and waited for me.

So I walked behind the counter and stood directly in front of him, inches away, between his legs. I reached a hand out, placed it flat-palmed in the middle of his chest. He didn't flinch or question, just kept gazing into my face, expressionless. I can only guess what my own face was projecting.

You must read on, Adam, there can be no turning back. And I must describe for you, at this important moment in my story, quite precisely what transpired and how it transpired and, if I am able, what it all meant. And while you may form your own opinion, eventually, you must assemble these facts that I am handing you like tools in a toolbox, you must lay them in their proper places, line them up until they all are there and you can make sense of them.

We stood like that for several minutes, I suppose. While he looked into my face I was assessing him: through my hand, which remained on his chest; and my eyes, which roamed from his baldness to his hazel eyes to his scruffy jaw to his thick neck to his chest, his crotch, his knees; and also with my nose, which was picking up his aroma once again.

I pulled my hand away, then using both hands I lifted the T-shirt over his head; he cooperated by raising his arms in the air and letting them fall when I'd finished.

With a flat palm again, I brushed my hand over his chest hair, his nipples, his belly.

He stared but did not move. I raised one of his arms in the air and thrust my nose into the curve, and I breathed as deeply as a man who has come up for air after too long in water. Deeper and deeper I inhaled until he filled my lungs and pierced my bloodstream, and then suddenly it had to happen fast. I rubbed my nose so the scent would stay there and I backed slightly away. I slapped my hands several times against his massive chest—he did not flinch—and with hands that shook (with desire, with impatience; there was no nervousness here) I undid his belt, opened the zipper and reached in to his already rising cock. It was as large as I had expected, larger even, thick and red with a huge head I could barely get my mouth around. I dropped to the floor and sucked in great gulps; he did no thrusting, was nearly impassive

as I lapped and kissed and gorged myself, my
eyes half-closed in stunned ecstasy. My hands
clutched his ass to push him deeper inside.

Until, without warning, he pulled my
head away, stuck his hands under my armpits
and lifted me in one swift motion to my
feet. He spun me around, fumbled with my
belt buckle until I understood and opened
it myself, and he pulled down my trousers
and briefs in a rough tug that caused my own
cock and balls to bounce into the open air.
I heard him spit into his hand and before I
could protest—I wouldn't have—or explain
that I had never been fucked, had only done
the fucking, he was pushing inside, that
enormous head of his too big, too huge, and
it was painful and perfect all at once, and it
was all I could do to keep from screaming,
though I moaned once, twice, bent now over
the counter, my nose to the cash register, the
gouges in the counter a design my eyes fixed
upon before they snapped shut so they too

could enjoy no distractions, and his hands—meaty, hard, calloused, how had I not noticed them?—grabbed my hips and he was pushing now, spreading me wider and wider and he was so far inside that I could feel his balls slamming my ass, and he was leaning farther back so that I rose to my toes as he pummeled and pushed and rammed and plowed and I wanted every centimeter of it and him and I wanted to stay like this, just stay like this, but I could feel him gaining momentum and now he was growling—growling!—and I was panting and he was pushing so hard that the counter I was gripping began to shake and for a brief moment I thought we might topple forward but I was able to hold on for one more battering thrust before he arched his back and pulled me into him and I could feel him spewing himself into me, and when he had finished and the throbbing had subsided I looked down and saw that I, too, had come, so that his orgasm was mine and mine was his and we were a mess, a heaving, sweating, panting, quivering mess.

And I was hooked.

I wish, dear Adam, that I could be sitting across from you as you read this. Is your pulse racing? Are other bodily changes affecting you? Through your shock, maybe your horror, are your eyes widening? Is your breath growing shallow and ragged? Goose bumps, perhaps, or a tingly scalp or spine? And how about your little *shmekeleh*? What's happening between your legs, and under your arms? Is your sphincter flexing itself? Are you thinking of Beth at all, or is she completely out of mind? It's all right, my boy. It's all natural, I promise you.

He took me into his house, where we showered and did it again. He fed me, then took me to his bed, where we did it again, then fell asleep, then awoke to another round at daybreak. We were matched in our insatiability. I could barely walk by morning, my throat was raw, my lips and jaw sore, my cheeks rough from his beard. I reeked of him. By the third or fourth time he was touching me not merely for his own pleasure but for mine as well. He kissed my lips. He stroked me, held me when we slept. We spoke only in the wake of sex, and very little at that. Who needed words when we were communicating with absolute precision and intimacy and understanding with every part of our bodies? Don't get me wrong: he wasn't a perfect lover, but even his fumbling or bungling satisfied me, and he was an extraordinarily quick learner who never made the same misstep twice.

I'd been drunk before, and hung over, but this stupor I walked around in for several days was a strangely wakeful one. Some of my senses were dulled, overtaxed, but others were heightened. I noticed colors with an unfamiliar intensity, and the scents of the spices seemed to reach into every corner of my brain and body.

My mind functioned enough to retain little bits of information, like the name of the place in which I found myself—which we shall call Kritmonia, from *Crithmum maritimum*, or sea fennel, a bushy flowering plant that grows on the cliffs that lead down to the sea—but not much more than that. Mostly, my days were spent waiting for him to be free—for an hour, for ten minutes, it didn't matter—so that I could consume more of him, fill myself with his juices, lap him up and tear into him like some maddened carnivore. I didn't know myself, didn't recognize this ravenous passion that felt more like famine than desire. Within an hour of making love I was starved for him once again, and he proved himself to be a banquet table, always laden with exactly what I craved.

I honestly can't tell you how long this lasted. I know he went to work in the mornings, ran his business. He had workers to command, deliveries to oversee, accounts to manage. He spoke on the phone, met with people. I watched from the edges, observed how he treated customers and employees alike with a benign gruffness that most people seemed not to mind. I hovered over him when he fixed things. I spied on him as he worked on the computer or checked advertising copy, curious what he was like when he thought he was alone. I scrutinized his face when I surprised him with my presence, though it seemed he was genuinely unsurprisable.

He was mostly happy to see me, or merely distracted—occasionally he would look up without seeing me, his mind still on whatever it was I had interrupted—but his happiness always contained desire, and I was always glad to find it there. Invariably it took only a matter of moments before we would be on top of one another, rarely making it to a bed or even a private space. In those first days we made love—if, in fact, that term applies here; I should probably coin a new term, something that is mostly physical but which contains the seeds of caring or friendship or affection or some other precursors to love itself—in the following locations: the spice shed, repeatedly; the storehouse; his house (the bedroom, the shower, the living room, the kitchen, the screened porch, the unscreened porch); a clump of low trees at the edge of his property, one afternoon when he was overrun with customers and we had to have one another right then; the beach at night, the beach at dawn, in the water, in the lifeguard's cabin; the front seat of his truck, the back of his van. Soon we would be making little trips for work or pleasure, and our lovemaking locales grew with every excursion.

I was drugged. I left my Hebrew classes, in fact I could barely get myself back to Tel Aviv long enough to fetch my belongings (and only with his help). I left my friends. I didn't speak on the phone or text, I barely emailed. I had little interest in food or exercise, none at all in television, unless it was watching a movie with him between lovemaking sessions. I was intoxicated to the point that the taste or smell of his semen was the only thing that could calm me down, before it fired me up once again. I had done some drugs before but never lost control; this was worse and better than all of them. I milked him dry, I milked myself dry, I heard myself as he bored into whichever of my openings he desired but I didn't recognize this voice of mine, the sounds I made, the way I begged—for more, for longer, for deeper, for harder.

And he, an ox, gave me what I needed without question or complaint. He came three, four, five times a day. He was showing signs of addiction just as I was; he lapped me up with equal intensity to my own mad craving. He feared no crevice or appendage, he kissed and sucked and fondled as though he had been waiting for this, only this, secretly as hungry as I was. He was unfettered, my wild animal led back to nature. And he was mine, and mine only.

This is the sum total of what I knew about him: That he was twice married and

twice divorced, the father of four girls and
a boy. That he had been raised on this very
piece of land. That his business was growing
but he wasn't making money. That he'd never
been with a man before, unless you counted
adolescent gropings with kids down the street
nearly three decades earlier. That he was forty,
exactly forty—twelve years older than I. That
he had never been abroad and had no real
desire. That his sisters had stopped speaking
to him when they understood he had inherited
this plot of seaside land on which they had all
been raised, while they were the beneficiaries
of their parents' meager bank accounts. That
his first ex-wife lived in the house next door,
the big modern place he'd built with his own
hands and abandoned when they'd split. (He
was too poor to kick her out; the only thing
of value he had was this property. With his
second wife he was smarter and made her sign
a prenup.) That he didn't know the exact dates
of his kids' birthdays or even their ages, unless

he did calculations that involved pinning them to events like the year the barn burned down or the year the chickens got Newcastle disease and had to be slaughtered. This was still before I knew that he'd never paid for a haircut or gone to a job interview or finished high school; that once he'd jerked off a dog; that he'd made several astonishing sculptures using old farm equipment and a welder's torch. And if I still knew this little about him, he knew even less about me, since he asked no questions, merely listened when I chose to recount whatever I chose to recount. But I was uncharacteristically mute in those days. My mouth was otherwise engaged.

If he was laconic about life in general he was nearly loquacious when it came to his farm. And although there were constant frustrations like money, organization and employees, he clearly loved his land and what it produced. Uzi grew herbs and Uzi grew spices, which I came to learn involve different growing practices

and have different requirements. The herbs
grew in long tunnel-like greenhouses on fields
he would ride off to each day. I had trouble
telling them all apart: dill and parsley and
cilantro and basil and chives. Fennel, lavender,
thyme. Spearmint and peppermint and a spicy
Moroccan mint I'd never tasted. Rosemary,
tarragon, oregano, verbena and sage. They were
constantly being harvested and needed to be
fertilized organically. The spices were even more
labor-intensive, needing first to be harvested,
then sorted, dried, ground and often blended.
He grew a decent variety of these, too, but
there were several he did not—like sesame and
sumac—and so relied on suppliers from around
Israel for those. And he took special pride
in growing edible flowers, like nasturtiums,
pansies, begonias, marigolds and Judas tree
flowers. I was disappointed to learn that two
of my favorites, cinnamon and vanilla, did not
grow in Israel. Sometimes in the evenings he

would take me with him to inspect the watering systems and he would always make me a cup of tea, never the same blend of herbs twice. And he would make love to me there and I would return home smelling of fennel and dill.

Although it seemed like a long time had passed—we'd already made love in one form or another probably thirty times by then—it was one morning less than a week after we'd met that the screen door swung open as we were eating breakfast and in the doorway, hands on hips, her long coppery curls streaming, the sun framing her so that I could not see the expression on her face, stood Nina, his first ex and nextdoor neighbor.

Uzi didn't miss a chew of his toast but I stopped eating and looked up at her. "So it's true," she said, staring at me.

Uzi poured himself some juice.

"You're screwing a guy?" she said to him, her eyes still fixed on me. "What's gotten into you?"

Uzi swallowed but did not look up. "He suits me," he said.

I wanted to jump into his lap. I knew enough of his silence to recognize a massive compliment when I saw one. I rubbed my leg against his and he dropped his hand to my crotch under the table.

"He suits you," she repeated, deadpan. "That's just lovely."

Nina walked into the kitchen, circled it. If she was looking for evidence of my presence or influence, there was nothing to find; I had changed nothing in the few days since my arrival. She turned her attention back to me.

"Who are you? Where did you come from?" She dropped into the chair facing me. "Mostly, though, how did you perform this witchcraft on my ex-husband? I mean, I know the guy pretty well and if there's one thing he isn't, it's a homo."

For the record, I didn't catch one or two of the words she was using. I've inserted *witchcraft* here because it makes the most sense, but to this day I don't know the word for it in Hebrew.

"Go to hell, Nina," Uzi said before I could respond.

"That's new, too. This guy also taught you to talk like that?" she asked. "Listen, Uzi, I don't care what you do with your prick but people are talking and we've got kids and this is a little weird. Since as usual I'm the one who's going to have to look after their mental wellbeing I'd just like to know what's going on here. Is this some passing fancy or have you really changed horses in the middle of the race?" She was on her feet again, her face reddening. "Uzi, I mean, what the hell? What is going on? You're the straightest, machoest guy I know. So what's happening? And what am I supposed to tell the kids?"

"Tell them whatever you want," he said. His voice was still soft but I could see something brewing. He had placed his hands flat down on the table as if to keep them from misbehaving.

"Listen, you," she said, turning her attention back to me. "I want to talk with you. Alone. It seems like you've moved in, and if we're going to live a few meters from one another and my kids are going to see you and hear you two cats in heat and maybe eat a Friday night dinner with you, well, I need to know who and what you are." She moved to the door, but on her way stopped behind Uzi's chair. She leaned over him, slipped her hands down his chest and let her hair fall around his face. I could see she was pressing hard into his flesh, maybe pinching him. "He's bad news, this one," she told me, her chin nearly resting on his head. "He gets that knife right up under your skin, I know, and once it's there he can twist it till you scream in agony." She slapped him twice hard on the chest, but this did not register with Uzi. "Come to my house at four, for coffee," she said to me. "But leave this guy at home."

At the door she stopped and turned back to her ex-husband. "Who'd have believed…," she said, shaking her head.

I had seen the children coming and going, and we'd eyed each other a few times with mutual disbelief. Obviously, for their part, a guy shacking up with their dad must have been downright weird. For my part, when I thought about it at all, I would wonder what kind of relationship they and I would wind up having. I'd figured out that the oldest, a thin zombielike girl in her last year of high school, was just a shade closer to me in age than I was to her father. So would we be friends? Would I be like an uncle? I don't have any nieces or nephews or little siblings for that matter, so I had no idea how that would work, or even if I wanted it to. Then there was a boy, only slightly younger, who was clearly well on his way to becoming as broad and manly as his father. How was I supposed to deal with him, and what would he want out of me? I'd watched him at the school bus stop one day harassing a boy his age and he seemed like a bully to me, the scowling, menacing kind whose mood you'd better watch out for. (I'd been like that myself for a period.) The third kid, a chubby girl with long blond hair and a pretty face a number of years younger than her siblings, had actually waved to me, almost clandestinely, one afternoon as she sat on the stoop of her house. Uzi's other children, two little girls, lived with their mother, Tamar, about ten minutes away.

Before I carry on with this story, Adam, I need to provide you with details of the setting, to give you a better sense of the place. Kritmonia was established in the early 1930s and Uzi's grandparents were among its founders. Its shining moment came in the late forties, when ships teeming with ill and weary survivors of World War II, considered illegal immigrants by the British occupiers, dropped their passengers at night on the beach below the village, and the villagers would hustle them inside their homes, dress them in local clothes and house them until new accommodations could be found.

Originally, everyone granted land rights to set up rural communities was expected to farm, but this village was so close to the sea that the earth was almost completely sand and utterly infertile. So the villagers built their homes on half-acre parcels of land by the sea while their fields were a tractor ride away, inland, where the earth was arable. Still, the citrus trees planted by the early farmers failed to produce the oranges, grapefruits and clementines grown so successfully in other villages. Most of Kritmonia's residents, like Uzi's grandfather, enjoyed far greater success raising chickens. The coops were in use until Uzi was well into his twenties, around the time that he started growing herbs.

Uzi's family farmstead sits on the east side of the lane that runs parallel to and closest to the cliffs; on the west side, atop the edge of the cliffs themselves, are a row of properties originally given to prominent Jerusalemites in the 1930s for the purpose of building summer homes. Those properties are now among the most valuable in the country, and the people who can afford them have destroyed all vestiges of the original modest cottages that stood there in favor of enormous marble mansions. Uzi was lucky in that the mansion opposite his property—the only thing standing between him and the sea—was built low, so the breeze and the views remained. He was lucky, too, to be sitting on an earthen gold mine, though of course he would never sell this land; where would a man like Uzi go? An apartment? Never. A home in a new development? Just as unlikely. And besides, he gave no thought to leaving millions to his children; I never asked him, but I assume he had no will. What would happen to this land and what would be bequeathed to his children after his death were of no interest to him at all.

Now, with his herbs and spices, Uzi made excellent use of all his lands, every inch planted and flourishing. He even rented extra fields from neighbors, none of whom farmed anymore, though he only paid them with produce, never cash. All day long he drove back and forth to his fields in one of his vehicles. There were several old buildings down there as well, rickety structures built and abandoned by his grandfather.

Slowly I came to understand that Uzi's forbears were bullies, large men and women with a healthy mixture of hearty Russian or Polish peasant stock good for intimidating the shtetl and city Jews that arrived in Kritmonia after them. They dominated the local council and pushed through resolutions that suited them and blocked the ones that did not. Several generations of neighbors feared them or despised them or respected them or all three. One disgruntled neighbor even informed me that the acreage owned by Uzi's family was formerly plots of citrus groves sold to European Jews in the 1920s but given away by the State of Israel after World War II when it was assumed these owners had perished; when some of them, or their descendants, tried to reclaim their land they were turned away—by the new Jewish owners and by the State itself. I recounted this neighbor's tale to Uzi and his response was a single word: *Bullshit.*

Uzi was often called on for an opinion on village matters, but I also noticed how some people would look the other way when they saw him coming, or speak to his face with a look of loathing he never caught on to. On several occasions I suggested inviting this or that person for cake and coffee after having a nice chat on the street but received no encouragement from Uzi, and the one Saturday afternoon I did invite a couple he was barely civil to them and I vowed not to repeat that mistake. He honestly believed he needed no one, no friends or neighbors. For Uzi there was only work and the biological imperatives: sleep, food, sex.

Kritmonia's beach was one of the most popular in the country; weekends and holidays brought the crowds. The day-to-day reality, though, was one of sand and humidity. Sand was everywhere, in all things. I could have swept the floors three times a day and still found sand in every corner. I adopted Uzi's bedtime ritual of sitting at the edge of the bed, raising my feet in the air, and smacking them together to keep sand off the sheets. The humidity meant all food left out went limp and stale within hours. I took to putting everything in the fridge or freezer, because even sealed packages in the pantry couldn't prevent food from going bad. Though for that matter, Uzi and I had highly different standards for what constituted bad food. A natural nonwaster of anything but most especially food, Uzi had also grown up in this climate (and this house) and was quite accustomed to eating wilted, moldy bread, for example. We never saw such things in the decadent, wasteful Beverly Hills of my childhood.

But really, Adam, I'm just telling you all this so that the picture you formulate, the backdrop you envision of my life in Israel, will be as accurate as possible. I want you to smell that salty air and feel its clamminess on your skin. I want you to taste those flaccid bread sticks as they melt rather than crunch in your mouth. I want you to experience the slight dampness under your palm as you smooth the sheets on the bed I shared with Uzi.

That afternoon, almost exactly at four, I knocked at Nina's door—the front door, the one facing east on Coral Reef Lane. It took a moment, but she opened the door instead of shouting for me to enter as most Israelis do. She did not smile. The kids did not seem to be present.

The living room was large and cozy, full of family things: art projects the kids had made, books and videos, pegs to hold the jackets and book bags hanging there.

The sofas were enormous and cushy. A heap of skates and skateboards stood in one corner. Nina led me to the back of the house, to the kitchen, and seated me on a stool at the counter while she arranged coffee and cake for us.

"It took me years to get him to build this house. Years to get us out of the one you're...staying in, his parents' house. God, how I hated that place. And then finally, when we'd finished building and decorating, we split up. I don't think he slept here more than a dozen nights." She was pressing buttons on a fancy espresso machine and the smell was enticing.

"He's a simple man, as you've already undoubtedly discovered," she said. "Instant coffee. No remodeling, that house is just the same as it was when I met him twenty years ago and that suits him fine. No wardrobe to speak of, just work clothes. Basically, in a man that's a good thing. His solid, steady male presence was what attracted me to him in the first place. But it's pretty extreme with him. I'm foaming the milk, okay? You take sugar?"

"Sure," I said. She had a good figure, I noticed as she moved around her kitchen. Her butt was small and round and relatively high on her body; she didn't have what was known locally as a "Mediterranean basin," the low, protruding, ample hips of so many Middle Eastern women. She wore a tank top that showed a nice pair of breasts. And that hair was amazing: full and thick, with auburn ringlets that burst to the sides and back and trailed well down her back. She clearly had been and still was a beauty.

"He never read a book the whole time we were married. That's twelve years. Just journals, agricultural stuff: *Citrus,* and *Record Yield.* Does he still keep piles of them in the bathroom?"

I nodded and she laughed.

"He never, ever changes," she said as she sat on a stool facing me, with mugs of coffee for each of us and a small plate of homemade chocolate cake. "Or so I thought. I mean, this is a surprise. You are a surprise. He actually succeeded in surprising me."

I said nothing, took a sip of coffee.

"I've read enough of the literature and seen enough in my work to know that this didn't come from nowhere, that it must have been lurking in him all along but he never let himself act on it. Or maybe he acted on it but never told me. Or...told you, either?" She was fishing here, reading my face for confirmation or denial, both of which I refused to provide. But I couldn't help asking myself if she was right. I'd assumed, and he'd confirmed in shrugs and grunted answers, that he had no history of sex with men. Later, as the fabric of my trust in him thinned and frayed, I would begin to wonder if I'd gotten this, too, wrong about him. But for now I could still delight in the feeling that my very presence was as powerful an essence as his was on me, and that it was I who had single-handedly ushered him into this new life to which he had had no trouble adapting because he was a natural, because *we* were naturally good together.

"So," Nina said after a moment. "I'm a social worker and I work up the road in Hadera, in the regional welfare department. Do you know Hadera?" she asked. I shook my head. "It used to be a cute little city until maybe fifteen years ago when the mayor made a deal with the mayor of another town farther north about who would get which new immigrant population. We got the Ethiopians and the White Russians. The other place took the Mountain Jews, the ones from the Caucasus Mountains. I don't know which is worse, or better, but we've got lots of problems.

"My Ethiopians keep killing themselves, killing their wives. Sometimes their children.

A man gets frustrated about work, or his wife's independence, and one day he up and slaughters her, often in front of the children and mostly with no warning. The Russians sometimes kill their wives, too, but their motives are a little different and alcohol is usually a factor. Oh, and I'm responsible for a few Arab towns and a Bedouin tribe in the area. Their specialty is honor killings. You know, a daughter has been seen sitting in a car with a man from another town, that sort of thing. Sometimes it's even the mother who kills the daughter, not always the brothers or the father. They're not too happy with gays, either, by the way. We had a case recently where the son who'd secretly moved in with a Jewish boyfriend in Tel Aviv was found hanging from a tree, his balls butchered off—clearly before he'd been killed, or maybe even the cause of his death, the huge loss of blood."

I'd stopped eating and drinking but Nina sectioned off a piece of cake with her fingers and popped it into her mouth. "Pretty stuff I deal with, eh?"

She was staring into my eyes but I gave no answer, just a shrug.

"I have three kids, and they have problems. Uzi is no help with that, never was. But soon he's not going to have a choice. Our eldest, you've probably seen, has an eating disorder that's getting worse. Sometimes she goes without food, but mostly it's the opposite: She eats in quantities you think could never fit inside her body, then she hurries off to the bathroom to puke it all out. At this rate she won't be able to do her army service, which might be one of the reasons she's let herself get so thin, I don't know yet. I'm trying to get to the bottom of it, but it's tough going. Her name, by the way, is Rinat and she'll be eighteen in a few months.

"Our son, Ido, can be a sweetie. Or a monster. He's mad at the world, which is not unusual for a sixteen-year-old, but I want to help him through this tough period and he could really use a father for that.

"Orya, our little sunshine girl, is already—I can't believe it—twelve. She's a delight, and easy. But I'm so preoccupied with the older two that I don't feel I give her enough time or attention. And she makes no demands."

This Nina, I was beginning to like her. She was straightforward, clearheaded. I figured she was a good social worker and a good mother, too, because she was caring and tough at the same time. Take notes, Adam: doing good for others sometimes means having to be a bit of a bastard. I enjoyed listening to her.

"So," she said. "Why am I telling you all this? Because I don't know who you are and you seem to have moved in and I have no idea if this is for real or not, but if it is, I need to know you're not a psychopath. I could use you as an ally, but maybe that's getting ahead of myself. Uzi doesn't just bring women—not to mention men—home. He was married to

Tamar for a little while—she's sweet, with about as much personality as a noodle—but other than her, he hasn't been in a relationship. We're talking *years*. I don't know if he goes out prowling for sex or just doesn't bother with it, but you seem to have appeared out of nowhere, and you're a guy of all things, and suddenly he's, I don't know, in thrall. And I need to know I can trust you, because he's still the father of my children and we still all live here together and not together. Do you understand? I need to know: Who are you?"

It was a good question, and one she deserved an answer to. I told her a little about myself and she asked the right questions that kept me talking even when I didn't want to; she clearly was good at her job. I gave her a nutshell version of my L.A. childhood, my Israeli and American roots, the garden-variety not-nearly-as-bad-as-the-neighbors dysfunctional dynamics of my family, and a bare-boned version of my abandoned studies and relocation to Israel. I expanded a small inheritance from my paternal grandparents into sums that would keep her from worrying I was chasing after money from her ex while still making it clear that I didn't have an actual source of income at that time. I turned a few former sex-friends into relationships. I don't know if she was relieved or more worried than before because her face gave away nothing. But the more I heard myself talk, the more I wondered. How, indeed, had I gotten here? Where was I headed? And, when I thought about it—and not for the first time— how had Uzi, a straight guy of forty, twice married, become a fantastic gay lover so quickly and thoroughly and freely, just as I had switched roles from fucker to fucked? Everything made sense when we were in bed together, but when I thought about it, it was too crazy, too impossible. These thoughts, of course, I did not share with Nina.

Right there, in her kitchen, I began to develop a theory. That maybe Uzi wasn't gay or straight, wasn't homosexual or heterosexual. He was just sexual: a sexual being. And for a male sexual being that meant plugging your dick in a hole—any hole—and wiggling it around until it left behind a deposit and pulled out. Simple, straightforward. He himself didn't seem the least bothered or concerned or curious about it all; one day he was fucking women, the next a man, but to him, it seemed, it was the fucking that was important. From his point of view there had been no change. Fucking was fucking, no matter who was on the other end of it. So which was it? Had I truly unlocked the chamber of his innermost soul, the gay man hidden under all those layers of socialization to be straight, or was there no innermost soul at all, just an excess of testosterone that cared nothing for how or with whom its master got his satisfaction? The problem was that the only way for me to know the answer to this question was to know who Uzi would choose to have sex with after me, and I didn't want there to be an after-me.

Matters were a little more complicated where I was concerned. I'd had plenty of men and not a few women, but all of them, I was now realizing, had been less diverse than I'd originally believed. I'd done the same exact things with them all, and no more. But with Uzi I was flipped. I didn't even want to penetrate anymore, it was all about me being penetrated, me being ripped open and invaded. I'd never moaned in sex like I was doing now; I'd always been coolly in control, no matter how great the sex. I wanted to ask Nina what she remembered about sex with Uzi. Had she craved him? Did she lose her sense of self as I was losing mine, wanting to be his, a piece of him, a part of him? And what, anyway, was so enticing about him? Like she'd said, he was no conversationalist, or intellectual, or philosopher. His power was entirely physical and sensual, and without any effort. I looked across at the woman who had once been his more wholly than I was, yet. How—and why—did someone abandon this

Garden of Eden? Was she crazy (and lonely, and sad, and sexually frustrated)? Or had she saved herself? As "happy" as I was, as much as I'd found myself in being fucked by Uzi, I knew there was something about him, about us, that was already consuming me. Could I remain me, remain whole, as it ate me from within?

Before leaving Nina's home I mumbled a few promises about being in touch, about helping with the kids, about keeping Uzi on track; she was surely smart enough to see through me.

Days were accumulating into weeks and I was going nowhere in every sense. I rarely left the village, though after a while I found an old bike and fixed it up. I took over the cooking, the laundry, the tidying, while Uzi came through with a squeegee and a rag every Friday afternoon and mopped the floors, the sand for once banished. He pushed money across the table at me and I used it to buy food, always

squirreling a little away for myself because I
had no job and no bank account. I tried, when
his big hand slid the money my way, to feel
like a housewife, like it was my job to take
care of us and his to provide the cash, but
I couldn't quite shake the feeling of being a
sharmoota, an Arabic word used by all Israelis to
mean slut or whore. The funny thing was that
while I felt uncomfortable about my status
at those moments, it was a different story
altogether when I was pinned under him on
the bed or the floor or the beach, or when I
was on my knees in front of him: then, I *wanted*
to be his sharmoota. It was rarely soft caresses
and feathery kisses I desired but the stinging
slap of possession. Ownership. My whole life
I'd taken charge: I was always the leader, the
dominant one, the guy who decided what the
group would order in a restaurant or what
time everyone would gather; the man, who
called the shots in bed. Now it was as though
I needed him to decide everything for me. I

was erasing myself, and while this felt vaguely humiliating in the bright sunlit kitchen, it felt as tight and right as his prick up my ass at all other times.

And if this isn't already quite clear to you, Adam, my guess is that Uzi knew none of this; nor was he trying to make me his sharmoota. He was just following his most basic instincts like any male of the animal kingdom. I'd never met any human being even remotely like him before, so wholly a piece of nature itself.

And yet, after some weeks, or maybe more than a month, the fog in my mind began to lift and I could see beyond the next fuck. I began casting about for something to do, something real, and it took no time or effort at all to discover that the answer was right in front of me: I began studying the herbs and spices that Uzi sold. I learned their English names, their Hebrew names, their Latin names, and their Arabic names, since some of his suppliers and customers were Arabs. I examined them, learning their physical properties; I tasted and smelled them; I read up about their uses in cooking and medicine. I went through Uzi's handbooks and guides, I searched online. I read and read. Uzi saw what I was doing but said little about it, though he clearly enjoyed the interest I was taking in his specialized little world. He would come sit next to me at the computer on occasion and quiz me on whatever it was I was looking at, but within moments he'd take my hand and put it between his legs and we'd be off again.

You know, I never once, in all the time we were together, refused that man. I could be pissed off or sad or distracted, but no matter what, my body would betray me and cave with his first touch. I never did figure out what the secret was, how he could gain control of me so swiftly and thoroughly. At that time, though, I wasn't questioning it. I was living it, and enjoying. Tell me, Adam, do you think Beth feels that way about *you*?

After a few weeks of intense study I began
looking for ways to put my knowledge to use.
I made new and improved signs for all the
produce. I updated his mailing list and wrote
English content for his website; in the evenings
I would read him what I'd written and explain
so that he could render it in Hebrew and use
it as well. I loved watching his thick fingers
grasp the pen, and when we were really trying
to get some work done I would have to pin
myself to the chair to keep from pouncing on
him. I began traveling with him, sometimes to
where the growers worked and sometimes to
clients—people who wanted to make an herb
garden, or restaurateurs who wanted to pick
his brain for advice. They asked us to sample
foods cooked with lavender or ras-el-hanout or
pickled black lemons. I started taking part in
the conversations. He never told them who I was
beyond my name. Quite often he fondled me
under the table or kissed my lips the moment
the devout Muslim in front of us turned to

serve us tea. I saw thousands of shekels change hands, no receipts.

It was in early August, when the weather turned too sultry and oppressive to get much of anything done, that Rinat, Uzi's eldest, began coming around.

I was cooking a lot then. Baking, too. Trying out spices and herbs. I used recipes I found in cookbooks and online, then I started experimenting. At that point I was still just learning, not trying to do anything with my knowledge; I just wanted to unlock the secrets these seasonings were hoarding. I'd always cooked—remember that elaborate dinner I staged in grad school, the chateaubriand with Calvados and crème fraîche?—but I'd never paid much attention to the seasonings before. It was riveting to me, and liberating somehow. It felt like I was getting to the bottom of cooking, to something more basic even than the ingredients. The seasonings became the stars of my dishes, and I was learning to feature them, which meant bringing them into the cooking process far earlier than I ever had before. I intuited which of them to grind, sauté or roast, and which method worked best for each dish. They were no longer an afterthought, but the raison d'être itself. They figured into the greater picture, too, of my wild lovemaking with Uzi. Just as his pungency was what stripped me of my senses in the first place, or more accurately brought them alive, so too did the herbs and spices I was gathering suffuse everything I cooked with an earthiness and sensuality I never knew food could possess. I swear there were times I wanted to bottle Uzi's essence and cook with it.

Rinat would show up at the screen door, shy and needy as a stray cat. She always knocked, even when I'd already seen her. She seemed to know when I was in the kitchen. We didn't talk much at first. Wait, that's not true. We didn't converse, but she talked, talked a lot. About not much of anything. There was a lot of nostalgia involved, stories of her childhood, when Uzi and Nina were still married. She recalled picnics on the beach and horseback riding and sitting on her father's lap as he zoomed about on his tractor. She liked to analyze her parents, too, sharing their foibles and strong points with me. I realize now that she never ever showed up when Uzi was in the house; I'll bet she made sure he was busy first, then came over.

I had no agenda with her, other than keeping good relations with the eldest of my lover's five children. I didn't try to be too friendly, or offer advice. I gave up trying to feed her; she rarely touched a morsel of food at our house in any case, even though I'd seen her put away an astonishing quantity of food at her mother's table. As Nina had predicted, Uzi understood nothing of his daughter's unhealthy relationship with food and refused to attend counseling sessions devoted to the matter.

When I mentioned the subject he sounded incensed, offended by what he perceived as her crime of choice: Let her starve, he'd say with a frown. It enraged him that she could consume large portions of very good food only to force them out of herself in no time. If he detested one thing it was waste, and this was waste on a grand and daily scale.

On a very hot day toward the middle of the month, when the air itself was so exhausted it refused to budge, Rinat showed up earlier than usual, as I, earlier than usual, was basting a chicken with a mixture of brown sugar, chile and mace I'd concocted the day before.

"They want to hospitalize me," she said with no warning a few minutes after she'd arrived.

I had just turned to the oven and was placing the chicken on a rack. When I got the oven door closed I took the dish towel that had been slung over my left shoulder, wiped my face with it, and slid into the nearest chair. She was leaning against the countertop, but when I gestured to the chair facing me, she dropped into it.

I looked at her for a long minute. Her face was round, normal and deceiving, but her shoulders jutted upward unnaturally, her arms were skeletal and her tiny breasts pushed delicately against her tank top, barely making a ripple. Uzi had once told me she hadn't gotten her period until very recently, and I could see now that she was still a child in spite of her age. She chose her clothes to emphasize that fact, and when I saw them hanging on the clothesline I invariably wondered who owned the doll that would wear them. I noticed, too, for the first time, that her hair was thinning. And there was no light in her eyes, as if she had looked to the future and seen absolutely nothing there worth striving for. The expression on her face was almost a caricature of hopelessness.

"Do you want to? Go to the hospital, I mean."

She shrugged like Israeli toddlers do, one shoulder pulled to the ear.

"Maybe it will do you some good," I offered.

"Maybe," she said flatly.

"I could use a little help, if you wouldn't mind," I said.

"With what?"

"Well, I've had an idea, and nobody knows about it yet." Indeed, I hadn't mentioned it to Uzi, who was the only person I was conversing regularly with at the time.

"What kind of idea?"

I thought I recognized just a glimmer, a tiny spark of interest, in her question. I don't know if it was the idea itself or being let in on what was essentially a secret. I didn't know, either, if she would run to her mother to expose whatever I would be telling her, but somehow that didn't seem likely. I already had the feeling she would be loyal.

"It's like this," I said. And I told her my plan. "Uzi," I said—I noticed she liked it when I removed him from fatherdom and made him simply this man we had in common—"Uzi seems to be sort of the king of spices and herbs in this country. I mean, everywhere we go people ask him questions about how to grow them or how to dry them or whether to grind them. You know, you've probably heard it all a million times."

She shook her head from side to side in slow motion and I understood just how little his children had been included in his world, his day-to-day life.

"Well, take my word for it, they all think he's God. The chefs, the foodies. The growers and distributors, too. But he doesn't make good use of that fact. He doesn't take money for consulting, he gives away all his knowledge for free. And worst of all, he stops short. Since he doesn't use the stuff himself—I mean, he doesn't cook, and he's pretty indifferent to all food—he hasn't put everything he knows into practice. And he never will, since he has no desire to spend hours in the kitchen or in restaurants. So that's what I'm trying to do, you see? All these cooking experiments are not just me learning but learning with a purpose. I want to help him become a food guru, too. Amazing recipes, let's say. Or advice on how to use these spices and herbs better. He's so close, he's amazing at what he does. But he hasn't gone far enough yet and I want to kind of give him that nudge. Do you get it?"

"Yes," she said. "But what does that have to do with me?"

"Well, I was thinking you could be a kind of sous-chef for me, if you know what that is. Help me cut and chop and stir. Give your opinion on color and texture, that sort of thing."

"Would I have to eat the food, too?" she asked.

I thought about that one for a moment. "It would be nice," I told her. "But I wouldn't force you. And even if you only tasted the food and spit it out it would still work."

Nina wouldn't like me saying that, I knew, but what *could* I say that would get this bag of bones to eat normally? Her trusting me was more important, I thought, than forcing food on her.

She brightened just a tiny bit. "It sounds fun," she said. "When can we start?"

"Tomorrow," I told her. "But early in the morning. This weather is too impossible for cooking midday."

Rinat showed up the next morning at six. I was putting toast and coffee on the table, wearing nothing but the boxers I'd used as pajamas before I began sleeping in the nude with Uzi. Uzi, dressed in work clothes, was in the midst of biting my ass when she knocked. He bit a little harder before removing his teeth from my flesh and his hands from my hips. I was slightly aroused and did not turn to her until it was safe.

"Eat something," Uzi said when she entered. She stood mid-kitchen in the ragdoll position she always took on, her hands limp at her sides, her feet forward and parallel to one another so that her jagged hips and straight-kneed legs formed a perfect rectangle with the floor.

She did not even shrug. I hoped she wouldn't bolt. "We're cooking today, Uzi," I said cheerfully. "Rinat and I."

He grunted, sipped his coffee, downed a third piece of toast slathered in butter. (This man put a loaf of bread away by himself each day along with half a cake of butter. Beth, with her vegetable crusade, would be appalled, wouldn't she, Adam.)

He rose from the table and without a word kissed me on the lips, with tongue, and slid his hand into my shorts; either he did not care what his daughter saw or, more likely, he was making a point of it, of me. On the way out he grabbed Rinat from behind, his huge arms encircling her, and planted a kiss on the top of her head. She closed her eyes, a look of pure pleasure on her face. I thought about how easy it was to win her acceptance of us, how ravenous she was for his love, how simple it could all be between them if it weren't so complicated. Uzi bounded out, letting the screen door slam shut as usual.

"Time to get started," I said as we cleared the breakfast dishes. "We're experimenting with lavender today."

For the rest of the month, Rinat and I cooked. We made potato leek soup with dried onions, saffron and parsley. We made braised beef with coffee and apples in paprika, ginger and cumin. We made sea bass smothered in my own take on Yemenite *zhoug*, a spicy paste made of cilantro, green chiles and lemon juice. We made rice with rose petals, sumac and sesame seeds. We made beef carpaccio with saffon, lemon and orchid root. We grilled chicken skewers basted with fenugreek seeds, smoked paprika and Urfa chiles. We made chocolate truffles with crystallized honey, star anise and cardamom. Not everything came out perfect, but most of it was fairly tasty and intriguing.

We dabbled in Uzi's edible flowers, too. Our creations included nasturtium soup, pansies filled with chive-and-nigella-seed homemade cream cheese, and meat and vegetable stews cooked with begonias, marigolds and Judas-tree flowers. Uzi ate all our experiments and offered pointers on what to change.

Rinat was genuinely a huge help. No task was off limits, from chopping to preparing meat, to scouring every pot and pan. And she was the one who came up with the idea that I should name my spice blends for marketing purposes. We had fun and a lot of laughs coming up with names for each three- or four-spice blend: Rinat wanted cocoa powder,

orange blossom and clove for herself; we
called a very earthy and local mix of oregano,
fennel, tarragon and basil by the name of Uzi;
Chitchat was our decision for blue poppy seed,
mustard and lemon; and my own favorite, a
delicate blend of rose petals, cinnamon and
cardamom, we christened Scheherazade. Rinat
began tasting more and more and sometimes
also swallowed. I swear her sinewy arms took
on muscle and she seemed happy, almost
constantly, in the kitchen with me. We chatted
about *ha v'dah*, as her father called it, this and
that, and her openness never ceased to surprise
me. I learned about her first sexual experience
(a botched and frightening attempt by an older
man from the village, whose name she would
not divulge); about how she would spy on her
parents when they fought or when they made
love (I wondered whether she was still spying,
now on Uzi and me); and she even, on occasion,
mentioned her food issues—how they'd begun,
how she coped, what she got out of it all. I

listened, never lectured. I passed almost nothing of this along to her father, though sometimes I suspected she wished me to.

With all the food we were making we needed diners, so Uzi's ex-wives and other four children became our regular guests, though mostly it was just Nina with Rinat, Ido and Orya. Our standard setup was to walk the pots and pans of food to Nina's house because it was more spacious and cooler—that house was air-conditioned—and because that way I wasn't stuck with the dinner dishes after so many hours in my own kitchen. Sometimes I didn't love the feeling of being an interloper into someone else's family, the five of them bound by looks and history, but Uzi, Rinat, and increasingly Nina made me comfortable. Orya—a happy eater if ever there was one— often seemed confused by my presence but was naturally bubbly and affectionate, while Ido often wolfed down his food and excused himself from the table as quickly as possible.

He began to fascinate me, that boy. He was Uzi as I had never and would never know him. As broad and thick already, with hair—sparse still, but clearly his father's—on his chest and face. Uzi of nearly a quarter century earlier: brooding, focused, quick-tempered. I caught him on the lam at odd hours, trying hard not to look shifty. He wore baggy clothes several sizes too large, just like Uzi, who could not stand anything that might encase him, but, like his father, the bulge in his trousers was unmistakable and I had to avert my eyes more than once. Don't get me wrong, Adam: I'm not a pedophile, I have no interest in children at all, let alone a sexual interest. But this was a man already, even at nearly seventeen, and not just any man but the prototype of *my* man, and I was constantly sizing them up together, noticing similarities in the jaw, the slope of an eyelid, the way they walked (a loping gait, as if something large was in their pants), the way they raised their heads and glared before speaking, and yes, their groins, how prominent their maleness featured. I noticed, too, how oblivious each was to these similarities, how little they cared about this connection of blood and bone and gene. I was only careful to hide my little obsession from Nina, who might explode if she thought I was ogling her son, and from Rinat, who was keenly perceptive and might one day quiz me on my feelings toward her brother much as she often asked sly questions when we were alone in the kitchen about the relationship between her father and me.

But do I make you squirm, Adam, when I mention the bulging trousers of a sixteen-year-old, a sort of stepson to me at that? Or that on the rare occasions I got to smell him and he wasn't wearing some adolescent form of deodorant but reeked of his own pungency, that his odor was quite precisely that of his father's, and I was intoxicated, and aroused? You're right, it's impolite. Worse, it's asocial, dangerous. But I'm being honest with myself and with you in these pages. So I ask you, with your crowdfunding for medical-care projects, don't you ever feel something sexual toward those sweet young things you're saving around the globe? When you visit them in Chad or Bangladesh, and they rush to thank you, gushing and effusive, don't you take them in your arms and on occasion think impure thoughts? Or maybe not them, maybe it's someone like the hot, hot daughter of that wealthy lawyer-couple on your board; she was wearing a *very* small black dress at the fundraiser her parents hosted for you and she kept linking her arm through yours and marching you around the room all evening as if she was forty and not fourteen. Anita, that was her name. I remember because I thought her mother introduced her as Lolita, and that seemed both prescient and cruel. So, Adam, what about her? First world, third world, it doesn't matter: you take one of them in your arms and she feels like Beth as you encircle her, or perhaps not at all like Beth, or she carries a whiff of her own sex.

And what exactly do you do with that? I know: you do nothing. You squelch it. You pull away quickly to avoid the touch, the friction. You shut that door in your mind, firmly. As we all do, mostly. But maybe, back in your hotel at night, the only light in the room the glow from the busy street below, you think of her, that sad-eyed waif, or the one with the perfect skin, and you can smell her scent again and then you touch yourself and then…but no, you stop. Not you. You detour to Beth, you think of Beth as you touch yourself and the game is over. It was that lovely local girl you desired, or the blonde in her starched school uniform; your soul wanted her and you denied your soul that pleasure. For this, no less than for acting on your desires, there is always a price to pay. So, enjoy and pay or abstain and pay? In my mind, there's no question at all which is the right choice.

But there was little time to think about choices or Ido or much else. I was suddenly busy, gainfully employed with cooking and learning. I quizzed Uzi each time he came into the house, sometimes stumping him for the first time. (I learned that when he ignored my questions entirely, as though he had not heard them, it meant he didn't know the answer. *I don't know* was not a string of words he was capable of uttering.) We were still banging each other hard and fast, but I often found myself thinking about some dish I'd made with cumin that didn't quite work, or what new uses I could find for cardamom, while he was humping me from behind. In October I bought a really good camera, a used Canon EOS with 45 and 90mm lenses perfect for shooting food. I took a few lessons with a well-known food photographer who lived one village away, and began shooting the spices and herbs, the dishes I made with them, the places where they grew when I visited with Uzi. I haven't shown you my work, but it was damn good. Spices in particular are very photogenic and easy to shoot, but I had a real knack for getting the light right, or putting them on some surface or in some vessel that helped show off their colors and textures at their very best.

By now, I was ready. One night, after a light dinner of couscous and black bass cooked with dried Persian limes that I'd prepared for just the two of us—a meal designed to keep from putting him straight to sleep—I cleared the dishes, poured coffee for us, and, before pulling up a chair and sitting down next to him, I took several sheets of paper from the sideboard and placed them in front of him.

They were in English, and I knew he wouldn't read them, but I wanted him to see how serious I was.

He glanced at them, looked up at me.

"It's a kind of business plan," I told him. He looked down again. "You know I've been working hard. In the kitchen. At the computer. I'm really into this." Weeks earlier I might have made a joke about working hard in the bedroom, too, and we might have vacated the table at once for the bedroom, or moved the coffee mugs and made love *on* the table, but at that moment I was all business.

"I've listed here the four areas I think we need to work on, you see?" I pointed to the paper, he followed with his eyes. "First, we make good use of the cooking and photography I've been doing. We can use my photos for better signage in the shop. That will make people buy more." His constant gripe was that people bought in tiny quantities and here I was practically promising him better sales. "But then I think we should do a kind of cookbook focusing on a different spice on each page. I've been working on it, I'll show you later. You won't need to worry about that part, I'll get it together and see if a publisher wants to produce it so it won't cost us any money. The cookbook will be in Hebrew and English. We can sell it here, but also online. And it'll be a kind of calling card. Legitimacy. It'll make us look like really serious contenders."

Uzi was silent, still focused on the page in front of him.

"A book like that will be good for drawing clients from overseas, and I think that needs to be your biggest move. After all, you're a total spice expert and people are looking for experts. We need to brand you as the go-to guy for advice from chefs around the world, just like you are already in this country." I was dropping more and more words in English into this conversation but since I had a pretty good sense of what he understood and what he did not, I knew he was comprehending everything I was telling him. In any event, I knew I had to keep it brief. Everything with him was like that: if you didn't get your message across in seconds, it was lost. So I pushed on. "The last aspect of the plan is marketing and exposure. I think we'll have to hire someone for that, but a lot of it we can do on our own. I've drawn up some ideas for that, too."

I stopped. It was enough for one evening. These ideas would have to sink in. I would have to wait a day or two, then ask him again. And even then his answer would most likely be monosyllabic but clear. I loved that about him. It was all so simple. There was no subtext. No guise or guile. His responses were clear and unburdened. Yes. No. Like. Don't like.

When he rubbed the top of his head he was sleepy. When he rotated his head slowly left to right, his eyes focused on something not in the room, he was working out a solution to some mechanical problem he'd encountered that day. When his lips parted in a kind of pant when he looked at me it meant we'd be having sex within seconds.

Everything with him added up neatly, which meant I knew how he would react to things and also how to manipulate him when necessary. He was no pushover—he could be stubborn as stone, and about as communicative—but to me he was like a limited series of buttons and levers, and when you pushed those buttons or worked those levers you invariably got the same set of responses. I became highly adept at knowing which combination to push and work for any given situation. I could play that man like an organ.

And what do you know, my friend? Are you surprised to learn that he went along with my ideas? Passively at first, merely allowing me my way and paying for things as necessary, but with more gusto later as he saw the bottom line, and the bottom line was good and growing. I took care first and foremost of the things I knew would most affect him, like new signs for the shop, and the design for a regular newsletter in two languages. But I was dogged about that book, and in no time I had a proposal together for publishers local and international. We met with experts in branding and marketing and we started making contacts with the press. It stands as one of my biggest regrets from that period that the book never got published. I worked so hard on it; eventually I completed virtually all the content and we were working on designs, and a few advance articles about it appeared in the press, which is when our publisher got a complaint about plagiarism—obviously ungrounded—sent on some Tel Aviv lawyer's letterhead, and the whole project sank in no time. I never even had the chance to prove my innocence to anyone, it was all just over in a flash. Uzi never talked about it to me but I know he stood behind me; why would I ever have plagiarized after spending all those hours in the kitchen testing my ideas?

Otherwise, though, a lot was happening with the business. Until that time Uzi had kept a limited staff of employees. There were two Thai workers, sanctioned by the Israeli government for jobs in agriculture. There was a bookkeeper, Miriam, a neighbor he shouted at regularly who seemed deaf to his complaints. There was Ruthie, another neighbor, who kept the shop running. And when Uzi needed extra hands he would drive down to Netanya and pick up day-laborers—Arabs from the territories or African refugees, whoever was waiting for work that day near the train station.

Now, however, this little team was insufficient. Business in Israel and abroad was picking up, and rapidly; the stream of cars making pilgrimage to Kritmonia was impressive. Uzi needed more help in the shop, more help with online services, someone to manage the four extra Thai workers he had just been allocated. He was busy interviewing, managing, directing, administering. Our days were longer and fuller than ever before. Now, I could tell, he too was thinking profit margins and press releases when he climbed on top of me and pushed himself inside. I was keeping track: we were down to making love five times a week on average, rarely twice in a day anymore and almost always at night, in our bed.

A true success story, no? And although it was built on his years of experience and knowledge, it could never have happened without my energy and excitement and drive. I poured myself into this life. I want you to remember, Adam, that it was I who caused this great leap forward, it was I who took the photos and came up with the spice mixtures and the recipes (though some, I admit, were variations on recipes I'd found elsewhere; variations, never stolen text). It was I who prepared the materials in English so it was I who brought in business from overseas. It was I who met with people, fronting the business for Uzi, who disliked long meetings and too much talking. It was even I who befriended emaciated Rinat, I who gained the trust of Uzi's ex-wives and his other children. It was me Nina came to when she needed Uzi's help.

I became the mainstay of this family and this business. Remember that, Adam.

I'd never been to Acre with Uzi but that fall he took me along for the first time. It's an ancient town that juts into the water right up near the Lebanese border, and when you step into its narrow alleys and cross under its stone archways and pass by its green-domed mosques and latticed churches you don't feel like you're in Israel anymore. Cleopatra had been there, and Napoleon, who failed to conquer the city in 1799 in spite of massive efforts. There had been a huge Crusader presence. Now it's Arab, mostly Muslim, and the most authentic Old City I'd seen. Uzi actually built in some extra time to our schedule so we could meander about the alleyways and markets and the thousand-year-old Crusader tunnel that runs beneath the city. We ate plates of hummus with chickpeas and olive oil at Sa'id's hummus joint, which was packed. We were offered coffee but Uzi told the waiter, "We're on our way to the Akkawis," and the waiter nodded, an acknowledgment of the excellent coffee that would be served to us quite soon.

The Akkawis, a family of Muslim Arab merchants who had been living in Acre for generations, owned a spice shop and business only a few meters farther on in the market past Sa'id's. Muhammad Akkawi, portly, dignified and wearing the thick salt-and-pepper mustache of most men his age, greeted Uzi warmly; in return, Uzi was more effusive than with most of our clients, or anyone for that matter. We sat in Muhammad's office behind the spice shop, a room of massive, vaulted stone walls and ceilings and thick rugs in patterns I'd learned had been popular during the Ottoman Empire. We were served dark, rich coffee with cardamom in tiny ceramic cups from a long-handled brass pot, and an assortment of the best baklava I'd ever tasted. I remember feeling ebullient. That's precisely the word to describe it, like I was filled with bright bubbles that threatened to lift me off my chair. Acre, Muhammad, the hummus, the coffee, the sticky-sweet pastries; I wouldn't have been at all surprised if one of the carpets had offered me a ride in the sky.

Most of the conversation between Uzi and Muhammad, for which I played the audience, was a recitation of mutual compliments. "Did you know," Muhammad asked, addressing me, "that Mr. Uzi knows more about nigella seeds than any Jew in this country?" "And did you know." asked Uzi, his attention on me, "that Mr. Muhammad has created his own special brand of turmeric paste used for topical infections?" They continued like this, one-upping each other in eloquent Hebrew for some minutes while I dutifully responded with vocalized and silent expressions of pleasure and awe.

A door behind me opened. "Ah," Muhammad purred, "here is my clever youngest son, Ibrahim, whom you and I have recently been discussing, Mr. Uzi." Ibrahim rounded my chair and in that brief instant in which he turned to face us, I saw it all: the proud, doting father whose filial love had softened his son; Ibrahim's sweet brown eyes, his shy smile, and his lovely, boyish body—slim hips, drooping shoulders, smooth cheeks; and, mostly, Uzi, I saw Uzi. He sat flattened in his chair, airless and deflated, as if some huge pipe had sucked the oxygen from his lungs. I might have dismissed this, might have thought I was imagining it all, but he clinched it when he turned his face to mine with a look I can only describe as guilt. Never in all the months I'd known him had I seen this look, nor would I ever see it again, since guilt was an emotion that could never be pinned on Uzi. But that one glimpse was enough. I knew it and I understood it. Now it was my turn to feel flattened, steamrollered.

But that was only the first shock. The second came when it turned out Muhammad and Uzi had worked out an apprenticeship for

Ibrahim, to be carried out on *our* property, in *our* spice shop, in what amounted to *our* home. Ibrahim would be housed in the apartment Uzi had been fixing up at the back of the storehouse, unbeknownst to me. He'd been renovating under my nose and I'd been too busy to notice it. Ibrahim would be coming to live with us and Uzi, in return, would receive distribution rights for Muhammad's special turmeric paste. I was stunned into silence.

I can guess what you're thinking, Adam. That this wasn't our property or business or home, it was his, Uzi's, and he had every right to do with it whatever he wanted. Well, technically, you're right. But what about morally? I had been busting my butt for months, and the results were showing. In fact, the whole deal with Ibrahim had only come about thanks to the tremendous growth we'd been experiencing. Uzi could never have hired him or given him a place to live even half a year earlier, when he was still struggling to pay his few employees. Now his largesse seemed boundless, and I had not only been excluded from the decision, I had been kept from knowing the slightest detail about it. All this and quite a bit more was swarming in my addled brain for the rest of the meeting, so I missed the details of Ibrahim's tenure with us, what it was he'd actually be doing. I had been in a different, darker place, struggling to keep from expressing on my face what I was feeling in my—heart, shall we say? So when we emerged from Muhammad's office and shop I was clueless, confused, even a little dazed. What had transpired there? What was going to change?

On the drive home I was silent most of the trip, strategizing already, pulling back. I wanted answers—oh, did I crave answers!—but I loathed the idea of giving myself away too much. I did not want Uzi to see how very deeply I was affected by this, and anything I

might say could reveal that. So I chewed my
lip and gazed out the window. A churning had
begun in me, a black whirlpool I could almost
see and could most certainly feel. But above that
whirlpool my mind was clear about one thing
only, like a bright star over the sea: that Ibrahim
would be coming to us in a matter of days, and
I had to start making plans.

I had scheduled a cooking session with Rinat
the following afternoon and only remembered
it half an hour before she was due to arrive. I'd
thought to work on some nice herbed soups
as the weather was turning cold, but my mind
was not on soothing foods, and so we set
out to make a spicy chili with mace, several
kinds of peppers, and cassia-bark cinnamon
I had smoked myself. As Rinat chopped a
few cayennes and jalapeños and I stirred the
browning meat, she began to talk. My mind
was elsewhere—you know where quite precisely,

Adam: Uzi and Ibrahim, Ibrahim and Uzi, and what I was going to do about them—so it wasn't until I realized she was speaking about a man that I caught up and listened.

"...and his apartment is really cool. It's got like this massive sort of, I don't know, sculpture thing in the middle of the living room..."

"Who?" I asked. "Who has this sculpture thing?"

"I didn't tell you his name yet." She put down her knife and looked me in the eyes, I suppose for dramatic effect. "It's Erez."

"So tell me more about him," I said, trying to sound conspiratorial. "And not just about his furniture."

She sat down at the table, too preoccupied to continue working. "He's older."

"How old?"

"Older. I don't know exactly."

"Like my age?"

"No," she said, but did not elaborate.

"Like your father's age?" I persisted.

"I don't know how old he is," she said, giving his age away by failing to deny proximity to her father.

"Okay," I said slowly. "And how did you meet?"

"You're asking all the wrong questions," she said, scowling.

"So what do you want me to ask?"

"You can ask…" She fell silent, stumped. "You can ask about his personality."

"Fine. What's he like?"

"Really nice," she said.

"He sounds amazing," I said.

She pouted, or staged the pout of a four-year-old by sticking out her lower lip. I noticed her fingernails were painted candy-apple red.

"Why are you being so mean?" she asked.

"Why are you being so cagey," I retorted. I said *cagey* in English because I had no idea how to say it in Hebrew. She got the idea even if she didn't know the word.

"He's maybe a little old," she said.

"I got that. And maybe he likes little girls?"

"I'm nearly eighteen," she said.

"But you look—" I stopped short. I knew her well enough to know she would pick up and leave without a word if I carried on. "You look great, Rinat," I said, changing tactics. "I'm sure he finds you beautiful and sexy."

She might be perceptive about many things, but with outright flattery she was as easy to please as a dog whose belly was being rubbed. She perked up at once. "That's what *he* says! All the time."

How childishly gullible she looked in that instant, with her candy-apple nails and her baby doll clothes and her round, round face and her lopsided hair (she would shear off whole clumps, indiscriminately, when in certain foul moods). Suddenly I had no patience for her and cared nothing for the progress I seemed to be making with her, this blighted daughter of Uzi, the man who only the night before had jammed a thick and solid wedge of doubt into my consciousness. I didn't want to befriend or help her, not now. It was something else entirely that I was feeling toward her, toward Uzi at that moment.

"He sounds sweet," I told her. "He sounds like a good man."

"I'm so glad you think so," she said, sounding livelier than I'd heard her in weeks or months or perhaps ever. "I've only known him for eight days, and most of that only online, but I've got a really good feeling. Like, I told him I like jelly beans and he had a whole big bowl of them for me next to the bed."

"Yeah," I said. "Go with that feeling. He sounds like a great guy."

We tossed the ingredients into the saucepan and I doused them with Tabasco sauce. While Rinat would be plied that evening with jelly beans by a father figure with dubious intentions, her actual father would be eating chili that would sear his lips and roast his gullet.

Ibrahim moved in two days later. Uzi had furnished the small apartment with furniture he had been amassing in the older coop, the one his father had tended and was now the depository for sixty years of Israeli farm living—a giant ground-floor attic of sorts. For his part, Ibrahim brought pillows and bedclothes and several suitcases of clothing obviously prepared by his mother. I learned later that while his mother preferred to keep Ibrahim at home, the sheltered youngest son of the family and the one who would look after his parents in old age, his father wished him to perfect his already excellent Hebrew, learn what he could from Uzi, and in general glean business practices from the Jews by studying them up close. Ibrahim himself had little

interest in the business, but was too cowed
to say so. He was a good boy, soft-spoken, an
innocent—a mama's boy *and* a papa's boy—and
I really couldn't be sure what, if anything, had
or ever would transpire between Uzi and him. I
knew only that Uzi, that rake, had noticed him,
and I was on guard.

I should note, here, that our lovemaking
took a surprising turn. He had always been a
powerful force, but somehow he never went too
far, never used the full strength he possessed.
Now I was pressing him onward, coercing
him to let go, to free himself. To hurt me.
To unleash the animal in him as it had never
been unleashed before. And he was resisting.
Whether it was because he was indeed afraid
of hurting me or because of something else—
was he saving himself for someone else? I
asked myself—I couldn't know. But although
he appeased me somewhat by slapping my ass
or grabbing me harder, I could feel his hands
pulling back and I didn't like it. It made me

want his violence more. I was out to exhume it, wherever it lay buried.

Ibrahim was pleasant, charming even, in his very quiet way. He spoke softly, smiled bashfully—making you feel you had earned that precious smile each time it came—and was easy to be around. Now that I think of it, Adam, he was a little like Jake from grad school, which is funny because Ibrahim is an Arab Muslim with deep roots in the Middle East, and Jake was a blue-blood American. One side of his family was Mayflower material, remember? That was part of his problem, too much to live up to. Those patrician parents were the ones who fucked him up, you know, not me. They're the real reason what happened happened. Grad school was just the icing.

Anyway, Uzi put Ibrahim to work, though his precise duties were clear to no one. I think Uzi himself had a vague notion of a personal assistant who could help oversee the fields and the shop and take care of all the annoying little problems that cropped up incessantly. Uzi was clearly trying to remember to include him in projects he was engaged in, but I could see it took him no time to revert to his usual self—he dashed off to attend to things without thinking of anyone or anything, got caught up in repairs or deliberations that had nothing to do with the to-do list he'd started the day with, was short-tempered with the world. Still, I don't believe I was imagining that he was more solicitous toward Ibrahim, slightly more patient and forgiving than he was to his other employees or his children. Maybe even to me, I can't say for sure now.

But that was confounding, too. It could very well be that he was aware that anything he said or did to Ibrahim would make its way back to Muhammad. That a foul word or a slipped secret could jeopardize his relationship with the man who was the most important spice merchant in Acre and the key to doing business with that whole town and perhaps the entire north of the country. Uzi did not generally take such considerations seriously—he kowtowed to no one, never curried favor or tried to impress or even take other people's feelings into consideration. It wasn't exactly his fault; he was incapable of empathizing. I'd seen it with his long-suffering children and certainly with his second wife, Tamar; Nina was a different story, tougher. Like me, she had no expectations from him in that regard, knew precisely who he was and what his limitations were.

There was another possibility, though, one I was only starting to become aware of as I traipsed around the country with Uzi and met the people he dealt with, and that was Ibrahim's status as an Arab. Uzi was, as far as I could tell, both a rightist and a leftist when it came to politics. On the one hand he seemed to favor social liberalism—he was, after all, cohabitating with another man, though I cannot know if that was a deciding factor for him or if he even thought about that at all—but on the other, he was capable of making pronouncements about how to deal with bellicose neighbor nations that raised my eyebrows on a number of occasions. And again, in spite of his unusual home life, he was still considered by everyone around as a sort of Israeli good ol' boy, or "one of our own," as they called it in Hebrew. I tried sometimes to imagine what he would sound like if he were in an American context and speaking English: would he be the kind to refer to "Ay-rabs"? Would he talk about "them" like other Israelis I'd met, perceiving Arabs as a huge, faceless, hostile population living in our midst? Or would he stand up to such talk, set people straight, risk sounding like a bleeding-heart leftist?

These musings—new to me with the arrival of Ibrahim; I hadn't bothered to think about Uzi and Arabs before—made me wonder specifically about Ibrahim.

Perhaps, consciously or not, Uzi was in his own way being politically correct. I had trouble picturing an Uzi so thoughtful, or devious, or conscious even, but I couldn't rule out his uncharacteristically gentle demeanor with Ibrahim as his own private meting out of affirmative action.

So these were the options I was entertaining in those days to keep from believing that Uzi's behavior really stemmed from a festering lust for that boy from Acre, that Arab Muslim, that son of an important man, his new protégé or apprentice, Ibrahim.

And in case you have not noticed something else, dear Adam, I'll point it out to you now: my life had taken on a new interiority, which you should see clearly in the change in this narrative.

Do you notice its inward focus? Do you perceive that this letter, like my life at that time, has shifted in direction? Where just days earlier I was a driven man, propelling a business forward, outward, with my innovation and ambition, now I was turning that potent energy to matters far closer to home. Sure, I was still working for Uzi, still spending my days creating materials and new opportunities and avenues, but I was distracted, and at once I perceived that my productivity was on the decline even if no one else sensed it. I should mention too that the issue of a salary had never come up—Uzi handed me cash for whatever I needed from small (or large, who knew?) stashes he kept in crazy hiding places in the house, the shed, the garden. But suddenly I was thinking about the fact that I was working full time and more without earning a penny. While Ibrahim's status was clear—at least the monetary aspect was: free accommodations, a smallish monthly wage—mine was anything but, and growing more complex by the day. Worse,

I knew I could not broach this subject with Uzi without provoking a fight, a sulk, suspicion. I kept it all to myself and my mind whirred with more complications.

I wrote you earlier that Uzi would sometimes employ day-laborers—African refugees or Palestinian Arabs, the ones who crossed into Israel each morning in their dusty clothes carrying plastic bags of pita, olives, hummus and hard-boiled eggs. They hung out in groups, the Africans on one side of the street, the Arabs on the other, waiting for Jewish Israelis to offer them a few hundred shekels for a day of painting or cleaning or construction work. These men had government-issued permits, which meant they were usually over thirty-five and the heads of households containing many mouths, men perceived to have too much to lose to strap themselves into bomb-vests to be detonated in shopping centers or schools.

Ziad was one of them. He had Clark
Gable good looks ruined by a life of poverty
and hardship. Uzi would bring him in for the
occasional job, then grumble about the quality
of his work. But since the workload was growing
he couldn't be too fussy and Ziad seemed to be
around on a more permanent basis.

I noticed that Ibrahim wanted nothing to
do with him. In fact, if I'm not mistaken he
initially passed himself off as Abraham and
spoke with Ziad in Hebrew, even though they
shared slightly different versions of the same
Levantine Arabic. For his part, Ziad seemed
to take Ibrahim's superiority in stride. I don't
know if that was a result of privilege and
upbringing—you couldn't miss Ibrahim's good
breeding, or Ziad's lack of it—or of Ziad's
implicit understanding that he, as a Palestinian
Arab Muslim from the territories occupied by
Israel, was always, in every instance and every
situation, the lowest man on the totem pole.
Even the Eritrean and Sudanese refugees had

moved above the Ziads of the world in status, as Israeli Jews preferred to employ them over Arabs. *They work like dogs and won't stab you in the back,* I'd heard a neighbor say. In any case, Ibrahim was rarely in charge of Ziad, though when that did happen, Ziad made no show of resentment or belligerence.

Ziad was assigned to work with me for a few days, cleaning out a corner of the old coop we were planning to return to usable space. He was affable, chatty. Downright loquacious, in fact, in his laughable Hebrew. (Ibrahim, in contrast, spoke with fluid precision and almost no accent; when tired or upset he might substitute a *b* sound for a *p*, and he overgutturalized some sounds, but all in all he sounded thoroughly Jewish and Israeli—far more so than I, truth be told.) While Ziad cleared debris, I stood, hands on hips, making a few construction and design decisions.

"You have woman?" he asked me when he returned from lugging a particularly heavy metal sorting box.

"I don't," I told him, still focused on my own thoughts. Uzi and I never brought our relationship to work, except with the two Jewish female employees who liked to feel hip and liberal by asking (me) questions. We had no idea what the Thai workers thought about us, if they even understood, or the Arabs for that matter. I'd tried asking Uzi once about what Ibrahim knew but he grew irritated in an instant and I dropped it.

"I have eight children," Ziad said. "One *majnouna*, you know what means *majnoun*?" He rapped his head hard with his knuckles and made a crazy face. "She born no air." He demonstrated by gasping and I understood: a lack of oxygen at birth and this baby girl was doomed for life. With faltering language and a lot of flailing he showed me how she was blind and deaf and terrified of the world. His wife stayed home with the girl full time. The girl's best friend was a doll he'd found in an apartment he'd helped renovate. She clutched it all day every day, and when she needed to be bathed she staged a full-scale tantrum the whole time the doll was out of reach.

"What about your other children?" I asked, not exactly expecting a stack of photographs but at least a few words about each. Instead, he took out his ID card for me to read aloud the names and birthdates of each. Funny: like Uzi, he needed prompts to know how old his children were. I figured I'd be different if I ever had kids.

It turned out that Ziad was just several months younger than Uzi, a recent forty, though his hard life made him look far older. His eldest daughter was nineteen, already married and expecting her second child. The next daughter was married too, and the third, not yet seventeen, he'd promised to a thirty-year-old in a nearby village just that week.

"What if she doesn't like him?" I asked.

He didn't understand the question no matter how I rephrased it. Or maybe it was I who failed to understand his answer, which remained steadfast: She likes whatever man her father chooses for her.

I wasn't stupid or insensitive enough to try to counter that, or introduce some useless Western thinking into this ancient setting. So I was all the more astonished when this hapless, traditional Muslim father of eight from the village of Lebeth near Nablus asked, "You and Mr. Uzi like this?" and rubbed his two index fingers next to one another as if to create friction.

"What do you mean, Ziad?" I asked, hoping to evade the issue by making him too uncomfortable—or linguistically challenged— to restate his question.

He looked around the room as if hoping to spot a different form of his question in one of the messy corners. "You sleep Mr. Uzi bed?" he asked.

His unexplained curiosity put me on edge, but his creativity amused me. "We share a bed,"

I said. He clearly did not understand the verb, so I said, impatiently this time, "Yes. Uzi and me. Sex. Yes."

"Ah," he said, nodding. "Good."

Good? What was that about, I wondered. But instead of pursuing it, I said, "*Yalla*, let's get back to work," and without another word he set to his task at a good speed.

Nina and I rarely met on purpose. It was more like we would run into one another and linger to talk for a few minutes as we hung the laundry or walked on the beach. I never just popped in on her, unless it was to borrow an ingredient missing from a recipe; she, on the other hand, sometimes came by with a question, or something she needed Uzi to agree to and would enlist my help. But on this particular afternoon, when she pulled up in our shared driveway she came straight to our screen door, knocked, and entered the kitchen, where I was baking shortbread rounds with a variety of spices.

"Smells good," she said.

"First batch will be out soon," I said. "Join me for coffee."

She fell into the nearest chair, drew in and blew out a deep breath, and flicked her long auburn ringlets over her shoulder. "I'm worried about Rinat," she said.

The girl had been coming around less and less frequently. I had the vague sense she was miffed about something I'd said weeks earlier, though now I couldn't recall what it was. But anyway, she'd always been unpredictable with her time, her moods. I figured she would show up again when she felt like it.

"She hasn't been coming home nights," Nina told me. "And they called from school to say she's been sketchy about making it to classes. She texts me, so I know she's okay, but I don't know what's going on and it's making me…agitated."

"Friends?" I asked. "Her last year of school, you know…"

She looked pained, and it took her a moment to respond, her voice quieter. "She doesn't really have any, not to speak of. I thought you knew that."

I had removed the shortbread rounds from the oven and placed a few on the table along with two mugs. Nina didn't make any move toward touching them.

It seemed clear that Rinat hadn't told her mother about the guy in Tel Aviv, if that indeed was where she'd disappeared to. I wasn't about to betray any confidences. "How about if I text her," I offered. "Sometimes she talks to me."

"That would be great," Nina said, smiling for the first time. She broke off a piece of shortbread and tasted it. "This is wild," she said. "Is that…cardamom?"

"Yeah. And Yemenite cinnamon."

"Feels like we should be eating them on the back of a camel." We both laughed.

"It may be my fault," she said. "This business with Rinat. I'm not around a lot lately. I…I'm seeing someone."

"Nice," I said.

"Well, yes, it is," she said, smiling again. "He's…hmmm. How to describe him…well, no offense, but he's the opposite of Uzi. Communicative and caring. Expresses his feelings. Tells me I'm beautiful, that sort of thing. I'm eating it up because I've never had that before, as you know. Or…do you know? I mean, is Uzi different with you? I failed with him, never found those things in him, but maybe you…?"

I didn't mind when Rinat told me about her love life, I didn't mind when Nina shared her secret with me, but when suddenly the spotlight shone on me, I minded a lot. I needed to deflect.

"He's complex," was all I would say.

But she was caught up in her own narrative. "Maybe the biggest thing for me is his lack of male entitlement. That drove me nuts with Uzi."

I was genuinely stumped and couldn't hide my curiosity. *Entitlement* was not a word I immediately understood in Hebrew.

"You know," she explained. "The way men—most men—simply feel entitled. Deserving of whatever it is they desire. If I had to sum up the failure of my marriage to Uzi in a single word I think it would have to be entitlement."

My cheeks were on fire and I knew she could see it. Entitlement was familiar to me— I'd grown up in Beverly Hills, after all, and have probably acted a bit entitled myself on occasion—but suddenly realizing that that was what I was facing, that I was on the receiving end of it, hit me hard, and I didn't want her to know just how precisely she'd named the malady that was plaguing me as well. It was his sense of entitlement that had led him to bring Ibrahim to us without discussing it with me, his sense of entitlement that let him plow his way into my body whether I felt like it or not, his sense of entitlement that caused him to make business decisions that were good for him but no one else. The list was growing longer as I sat in a state of mute realization. His sense of entitlement would affect everything between us, always, because the only way to live with a person of such inflated entitlement was to deny entitlement in oneself entirely. And what was the opposite of entitlement? *Disenfranchisement* was the first word that came to mind, and it clearly fit me like a tailored suit. I was disenfranchised from friends, family, America, grad school, and now, if this makes sense, my relationship with Uzi ever since Ibrahim had come on the scene.

Nina seemed to understand I needed to be alone and after a moment stood up to leave. I mumbled something about wishing her luck and hoping to meet her man-friend one day soon.

"I'm sure you will," she said, "though I'm not looking forward to introducing him to Uzi.

And thanks for offering to talk to Rinat. Please let me know. I'm really worried."

"Sure," I said. "Sure."

Uzi was working longer hours than ever. He was away more, too, out of reach. Where once he would pop home for food and sex at odd hours of the day, now he was often inaccessible. He might be buried under paperwork in his office, or instructing his workers, or running around the country on errands I knew nothing about anymore. I rarely accompanied him; Ibrahim often did, it appeared, because I would seek him out when Uzi's pickup truck was gone, rarely finding him. Uzi often didn't answer his phone.

I was still cooking and baking now, too, and sometimes I concocted cocktails or frothy desserts. I got wilder with my spices, more daring, but each time I thought I'd certainly

put people off with my bold combinations
and frankly mismatched flavors, the more
people praised me. I began paying closer
attention to the measured quantities and was
gaining prowess in pairing my mixtures with
certain foods—and not necessarily the foods
commonly associated with those spices and
herbs: mushroom omelet with cumin and
saffron; roast turkey with lemongrass and palm
sugar; baked financiers with smoked cinnamon
and paprika; verbena, white cardamom
and sage on poached pears. After a highly
successful taste test with journalists set up
by our marketing and branding consultants,
articles of praise began appearing in print and
electronic media, and the effect was immediate.
Television beckoned, women's magazines,
weekend supplements for all the big papers.
Our customer base grew and grew. Individuals
were flooding the shop, restaurants were placing
bulk orders. It was as though the world had
awakened to spices and we were the sole address.

Uzi lost his cool a few times from the pressure, but mostly he was pleased without ever saying so. He took on more employees for the shop; I didn't even know all their names anymore. He jumped from bed earlier, returned later. We were now exclusively making love at night, probably three times a week. My thoughts about the possibility he was doing the same with Ibrahim dissipated. We were all too busy for such nonsense, that much seemed clear. Uzi, I believed, had been tamed in a sense. We were gentler with one another. We kissed more. I could lie stroking the hair on his chest for an hour before falling to sleep without enflaming him, or myself.

Odd though it seems now, I never even thought to look at his phone. So one day, when he'd forgotten it on the table after breakfast, it was almost as an afterthought that I picked it up and started pressing buttons. There were hundreds and hundreds of phone numbers, usually saved in random, idiotic and misspelled ways only he could understand, like Champinyon Negev or Best Safron in Galilee. There were names, mostly men's, with odd assortments of numbers after them: Nadav17668, Miki21, Ori18071. When I heard his footsteps approaching I returned the phone to the table and carried on with clearing the dishes.

After that, I took every opportunity to learn it. He used an old model I wasn't familiar with, and I never had much time until one evening I was able to sneak it to another room while he slept and I sat down determined to expose the phone's secrets. Until then I'd focused on the address book, but that evening I had a new goal: message chats.

I found cryptic conversations there with Ibrahim. *Ready?* came a message from Uzi; *RUFree?* was another from Ibrahim; and this, from earlier that same day: *Potting shed@1700.* The potting shed, at the far end of the property, was mostly where the Thai workers labored, but by five o'clock they'd have knocked off for the day. Where had I been at five, I wondered. What silly task had I been fulfilling when they were coming together not fifty meters from where I was standing?

By then, my heart was pounding furiously, my ears were burning, my hands were shaking. Not trembling, but shaking so hard I could barely hold the phone steady. Something was obstructing my throat, and it felt like my heart itself—huge, bloody and wounded. I thought I could feel the blood pulsing through my veins and it was hot, molten. Was that a car siren I was hearing or a scream in my own head?

You'll think I'm exaggerating. But no, my friend, I'm not. Within seconds of this revelation, my whole body was reacting, and hugely so. I ran to the bathroom and things poured out of me from every orifice. I'd never have believed I could produce so physical a reaction to so emotional an event, but there I was after five minutes or twenty, my cheek

pressed to the cold tiles of the bathroom floor,
soiled and gagging and breathing raggedly,
the phone lying lamely nearby. When I could
breathe and think again, I picked myself up,
threw on a tracksuit, and ran down to the
deserted winter beach, where I shouted at the
top of my lungs and kicked the sand and threw
any rock or shell I could get my hands on. But
it wasn't hurt and sadness I was screaming at
the waves, it was a fury so deep and fiery and
blinding that before that moment I could not
have imagined any human being could contain
such ugliness.

And now that human being was me.

I did not sleep that night. When I was spent
on the beach I climbed back up to the house,
brushed the sand off as best I could, wrapped
myself in a blanket and sat on the porch. It took
a while, but eventually the noise in my head
subsided and I could think clearly, or think at
all. And with that sliver of clarity I made a few
resolutions:

(1) I would discuss nothing of this with Uzi. In matters like this, as with so many others, I could predict his response. He would grow instantly angry that I'd been prying, tell me my suspicions were ungrounded and paranoid no matter what the evidence, and clam up. I wouldn't get another word out of him. Apologies or contrition were completely out of the question, they were nonexistent in his range of responses. I would be alone with this; that much was clear.

(2) I would mention this to no one else. Not a hint to Nina, who would be sympathetic and righteous and not a little smug, relieved to have survived him, relieved for the vindication, relieved to be in a different type of relationship with a different type of man, and I would not be able to handle watching her step lightly from my kitchen, as if my burden had become her unburden; nor would I mention this to Rinat, who, in spite of her long history of desperately willing her father to be the father she needed,

would side with him in a flash; and there was no one else, I suddenly realized, because I had long since abandoned all semblances of friendship with the people I knew from Tel Aviv and hadn't bothered finding friends since coming to live with Uzi. And anyway, how could I possibly share this humiliation with another soul?

(3) I would gather more information. I would check his phone as often as possible and record his interchanges with Ibrahim. I would look for patterns—when was he slinking off, what times of day, how often. I would go into his computer; maybe he had expanded to online hookups with other guys. I would follow him, track him, hunt him down.

(4) I needed money of my own, but asking for a salary would only complicate matters and piss him off. I would have to find other ways.

Dawn was fast approaching and I felt better having a plan, shaky as it was. There was just one thing that wasn't at all clear to me at that point: how I would manage to go on living with him, cooking for him, looking after him, having sex with him. Smiling at him. Asking him about his day. Working with him or, as I now saw it, for him. After all, I had been busy helping to fill his coffers like a good helpmeet, but what was I receiving in return apart from a roof over my head, food in my belly and a warm body next to me in bed? Was this really a man, a relationship, I could rely on for a future, for permanence? What if one day I wanted children? Or to develop my career in other ways. How supportive would he ever be of any part of me that existed outside his world of spices and this sandy piece of property—highly valuable, I might add, and not worth a cent to me? Damn that Nina. Ever since she'd planted the word *entitlement* in my head it was as though I saw it emblazoned on Uzi's forehead at every moment of the day.

It's not an easy thing, you must be thinking, Adam, to make such decisions about the person you love, or thought you loved, and

yes, I'd been playing with that word and had
used it with him on more than one occasion,
soliciting a grunt in return, or more often,
renewed ardor (that prick, hard in an instant,
always ready, always ready), but never the words
themselves in return. I suppose he thought his
hardened prick *was* the answer, *I love you* in its
purely physical incarnation. Or, more likely, he
gave it no thought at all. As was so often the
case—here, the evidence: the phone!—he was
all instinct, all animal, all physical. His brain
or his soul never kicked in, guilt had no status.
He desired, he took. Things I'd read recently
flooded my mind, the connections sizzling
like live wires: how men needed to spread their
seed as far and wide as possible; it was only
biology after all, and here was Uzi, a man as
close to nature as men get. He couldn't help
himself! Nature's imperative was causing him
to fuck, to fuck, to fuck again. Or this one:
that autism is an extreme form of maleness
and shares many of its characteristics. Uzi,

as male as they come, was indeed oblivious
to the needs of others, incapable of empathy;
I'd seen that time and again, most notably
with his five children and two wives. Oh, how
everything was making sense, fitting together! I
saw it all now, how such a man could fall into
a relationship with me. Where once I'd lauded
his daring—the way he'd taken on a male lover,
installing me in his house in defiance of his
ex-wife and children, raising his middle finger
to middle-class morality and the ogling eyes of
neighbors—now what I saw was a selfishness so
thorough and so pure that there was no room
for others at all, except as accessories, or, like
me, as a handmaiden to even more selfishness
(I provided sexual services, maid services,
international communication, editing, fetch
this fetch that, the list is endless), so that the
opinions of others had no voice whatsoever. It
was how he ran his business and how he ran his
life. Ultimately, in Uzi's life there was no one
but Uzi, morning, noon and night.

What a fool I'd been, I saw now, to have expected more. To have believed myself so central to him, so important. I thought I was the conduit between him and the world, but in fact I was his facilitator. And I'd done my job perfectly, making him a comfortable home life, providing sex always, moving his business forward with great strides in very little time and for a very small financial investment. What an ass and an asset I'd been! And he "loved" me because what I wanted was always precisely what *he* wanted, and no more. Had I ever, really and truly, tried to push my own agenda on anything? Oh sure, I'd gotten him to agree to buying a fancy camera (used) and better software, and to financing a marketing expert. But those were all ultimately for him, to enhance him, whether he initially understood that or not. Had I ever, even once, pushed for something wholly, selfishly my own? I couldn't think of a single thing.

You're right though, Adam: drawing these conclusions about a loved one is highly unpleasant. You can't imagine thinking such things about Beth, and, for all her faults, which I'm only too happy to enumerate, you're right in thinking that it couldn't happen with her. Or most any woman, in my opinion; they simply don't have the same level of entitlement. Ironically, too, I swiftly realized that all the things I admired about him, or outright adored, were the very things that had gotten us to this impasse: his independence, his nonchalance, his masculinity, his forbearance, his steeliness. How, I wondered, could I love these characteristics one day and loathe them the next?

You're wondering, I know, why I didn't just pick up and leave when I found that phone. Ah, well, remember this, Adam: I had been less than a year in Israel. I had no job and no home other than what was provided by Uzi in all his munificence. I had no friends, no real prospects. I was suddenly a 1950s housewife, trapped and helpless.

But there's another, darker reason. I had a purpose now, a job to do. I was not going to skulk, I was not going to slither off and disappear under a rock. I'd given myself to him wholly and I was going to take back something in return. What exactly that something was was not yet clear to me, but I knew for sure it was going to cost him dearly.

Rinat turned up mid-morning the next day in the midst of a cloudburst, that winter's first. I was watching the rain sluice down the spice shed, idly wondering where Uzi was and whether I should try to find him, when she entered dripping rain and shivering. Since her house was only a few feet away I knew she must have been out somewhere to have gotten that soaked, but she mentioned nothing of that. We'd been texting almost daily, but mostly just checking in with one another, nothing substantial. I made her a frighteningly strong cup of black coffee, the way she liked it, and brought her a blanket and a tracksuit of her father's that he wouldn't wear because it fit him too snugly. I knew the tracksuit would make her happy: Nina, Rinat and I all loved wearing Uzi's bulky cotton clothes, a fact he complained about each time he reached for an article of clothing that wasn't there.

There in the kitchen Rinat stripped to a pair of tiny pink panties and lace bra, which would have passed for what was once called a starter. Her body was full of hollows and shadowy indentations, and I couldn't be sure I wasn't looking at a few bruises as well. She took no pains to hide anything, so I figured the topic was open for discussion.

"Your mom's worried, you know," I said. "And from what I can see, she's right."

"I bruise easy," she said, stepping into the sweats so that her body was swallowed up and gone, lost in yards of deep green fabric.

"Still. You're a minor playing with a major leaguer." That little pun didn't precisely work in Hebrew, but she understood.

"For the record, I'm not officially a minor anymore. Eighteen last Tuesday. You forgot." She pouted but her eyes remained merry.

I leaned in and kissed her on both cheeks. We sat. "Happy birthday, hon," I said. "Eighteen. Wow."

"I'm officially never going to be a soldier, either," she informed me, quite cheerful now. "Got my papers and everything. I'm a whopping five kilos under the minimum."

"I wouldn't be so proud of that if I were you."

"Whatever." (She said this in English. A new affectation picked up in Tel Aviv.) "Next I'm going to try for a handicapped sticker for my car. Sometimes walking can be pretty hard on me."

Always, with Rinat, I alternated between wanting to hug her and wanting to smack her.

Just eat normal quantities, I longed to say, and let your body digest and benefit from them. Just eat and you won't be a cripple anymore. But these months with her had taught me that she wanted to be a cripple, that she wanted to be a dependent ten-year-old no matter what her real age. When Nina had begged Uzi to intervene with regard to this much older man Rinat was practically living with, Uzi had actually said he was happy some other man would be taking care of her instead of him. Nina had said, "You're a selfish pig, Uzi. Once again, no help from you," and she'd stood up and marched out with not a glance at either of us. My first thought had been of Ziad, the "primitive" Muslim from the territories, marrying off his daughters to the highest bidders. Was this really any different?

But to Rinat I made sympathetic faces and cooed encouragement. She talked about living in the city—she wasn't even attending school much anymore—and how she spent her days languishing in his apartment or walking his dog in the various parks, waiting for him to come home at the end of his long days as an accountant. He was forty-six, she let slip, older even than her father, a lifelong bachelor with an apartment he owned, not rented, in a new building a few blocks from the sea on Bograshov Street. He was a vegan, wanted the place kept meticulously clean, loved his pug and his Audi and sex with very young women. He loved her, she told me, her eyes clouding, as if I were about to deny it. He told her often. And he showed her, by buying her lots of clothes and taking her to fancy restaurants and bars, though never to meet his family. He had plans to take her to Amsterdam.

"And he thinks I should get into film."

I didn't understand at first. I thought the Tel Aviv University film school, or some private institution where she could study since she wouldn't be serving in the army. But it soon became clear he wanted her in front of the camera, undressed, and getting it on with other girls and boys just old enough to be legal but with the looks of children several years younger. "Pretty cool, don't you think?" she asked me.

There it was, this question, lying on the table in front of us, and it could not be ignored. I'd been listening all along, wondering at the innocence of this barely-eighteen-year-old in the hands of a creep. How had she fallen so far off the path, so quickly? And here she was telling me, only me, I was quite certain, and in effect asking my approval. Or, more accurately, my help. Her cheery presentation of the facts was really, I could see with absolute lucidity, a drowning girl's cry for salvation. Tell me I've got this all wrong, she was saying. Tell me not to dress like that, not to act like that. Tell me not to go back to Tel Aviv, to him. Lock me in my room and turn me back into the sweet little girl I once was, the girl who made elaborate art projects for everyone's birthday, some still hanging in her mother's kitchen.

So, Adam, she was handing me her life, and no less, as we sat in her father's kitchen with rain falling all around us. But before I tell you how I handled it, please remind yourself of these facts: I had only the night before received actual proof of Uzi's infidelity, his cruelty toward me and the depth of his selfishness. I hadn't slept at all and I was too agitated to eat. My head was swimming with plans and thoughts and too much noise. And I was volatile as an exploding bomb but without a clear target yet. I only knew I must hurt him. All those hours spent cooking with Rinat, the slow progress I had made with her and the edgy joy she seemed to be accruing, meant nothing anymore; they were gone, with Uzi to blame for it.

"You know something?" I said slowly, as if I'd been pondering what she'd asked me. "It does sound cool. Liberating. I always say, bite off life by the mouthful and chew it with gusto."

She smiled wanly. "So you think I should do the movie?" Her eyes were begging with me, shouting, pleading with me to stop her.

"Absolutely," I said as I spread my lips wide into what I hoped was a warm smile but which felt like a sneer. I cupped my hands over her small, cold ones on the table to close the deal, as if we were shaking on it. "Do it, Rinat," I commanded, probably with the precise sharpness of tone her boyfriend used with her at moments like these.

I'd been talking to Uzi for weeks about turning one of the old buildings down by his fields into an alternative site for the shop, which was quickly outgrowing the area of the house and becoming a nuisance to the neighbors with traffic jams and noisy customers, a place we could also use for events, like tastings or private parties. He kept telling me we had to wait for the first rains to check out the state

of the roof, so when the downpour stopped
and the sun came out I took the bike from
where it was leaning against the porch and rode
off. The normally sandy paths were easier to
maneuver, except for a few places where puddles
had formed. I didn't care. It felt good to be
out, the sky was clean, the air bracing, and the
usual smell of salt was gone, if only for a little
while. It was a good distraction, too, to leave
the house; I was restless, full of nervous energy,
unquiet. And I had an ulterior motive as well,
which was beginning to be my modus operandi:
I wanted to see if Uzi was using those old
buildings for trysts.

I was surprised to hear noises from inside the
oldest of the buildings, the one I thought would
best serve our purposes and was least used, or not
used at all. My heart was thumping, but there
were no vehicles around so I couldn't understand
who might be there, if anyone. There were no
windows into which to peer and when I tugged
gently at the rusty door it was clearly bolted from

the inside. I stood behind a cabinet to the left of the door, noiseless, listening to the occasional scuffle or rustle.

Clearly someone was in there, though no words were being uttered. After ten minutes or so I heard the bolt sliding back and the door creaked open just a tad, then fully. Ido emerged. Before he could latch and lock the door from the outside, I stepped out of my hiding place, nearly toppling him. I stuck my foot in the door so he couldn't close it.

"What do you want?" he asked with a scowl. I was impressed how quickly he'd recovered from the shock of being caught, and how as usual, though he'd hate to hear it, his response was just what his father's would be. He'd clearly be an expert at entitlement in another few years, if he wasn't there already.

"I want to know what you're up to," I said, wedging my body inside.

"Don't go in there. You have no right," he said. He was trying to be menacing but I wasn't having it. I was taller, older, and he was clearly hiding something.

"Nor do you," I said. "Especially with what you're up to."

He said nothing.

"Do you want to show me or do I have to tear things up to find out for myself?"

He thought for a second, his eyes roaming just as Uzi's did when thinking. I know the calculation he was making: *This dude is my dad's faggot whore and he wants us to be buddies so if I'm nice and I show him he'll keep my secret. If not, the homo might just rat on me.*

He entered the building with me and turned the light back on, then bolted the door behind us.

There was nothing remarkable here, nothing eye-catching. I give the boy credit for his stealth. It was unlikely even Uzi would have noticed anything out of place.

Ido, broad and bulky in the baggy jeans all the boys were wearing, led me to a very old and unremarkable desk with three drawers that had been turned to face the wall, only a small space separating the two. We wedged ourselves in and he pulled a key from a ledge near the ceiling, then fitted it into the top drawer. It was large and deep and filled with small packets, neatly wrapped and labeled.

"You're a drug dealer?" I asked. "You sell to the kids at school?"

He grinned, and I could see this was a source of pride. He was actually quite happy to be showing me his stash. What good, after all, was success if no one knew about it?

"My client base is a lot bigger than just schoolkids," he told me.

The bags were labeled, I could see, but in code. I yanked open the second drawer and found his notebook.

"No peeking," he said.

I'd seen enough. We stepped out from behind the desk and he locked the drawer and returned the key to its hiding place.

"You must be making a small fortune," I said.

"Yup. Gonna buy my way out of here just as soon as I can."

"Good for you," I said.

I was positioned in front of the bolted door, and when he made for the light, as if we were leaving, I put my hand out to stop him.

"I know your secret now, Ido. I can bring you down." I said this with a smile.

He mirrored my smile, and I saw on his face just how serious we both looked. "Maybe," he said.

"Your mom would send you straight to juvie," I said, using the English word I knew he'd know from television, "and your dad, well, he'd probably cut you off or something. Turn you out."

"Fuck him," Ido said, still smiling.

"But all those clients going down with you, well, that would be a tragedy you'd pay for forever, wouldn't you?"

"What do you want?" he asked, no longer smiling. It was remarkable, really, that a sixteen-year-old—or was he now seventeen?—was savvy enough not only to run such a business but to understand that a deal was about to be struck.

"Not much at all, really," I told him. "I'll keep your secret, every bit of it. You can maintain your business and keep that cash coming in."

"You think I'm giving you a cut?"

"Don't be a rude asshole, Ido. If I wanted a cut you'd have to give it to me, and with a smile."

"So what do you want?"

"Pull down your pants," I told him.

"Fuck you, homo," he said.

"Pull them down, Ido, you little fucker. All the way to your ankles."

"You're sick," he said, and tried to make for the door.

I grabbed his wrist and twisted it. "I'm not going to hurt you," I told him. "And I'm not going to make you do anything. All I need is a little information. Closure. So do it now, do it fast, and we can both go home and forget about this."

I released his wrist and he stepped away from me, clearly shaken. He stood facing me, breathing heavily, and he was beautiful, more beautiful even than I'd noticed. *Perfect* was the word that roared into my mind; how had I not seen that he wasn't just handsome or well formed: he was perfect. Every single feature was the best of its kind, and so was the composite.

He just kept staring, waiting for me to relent, but I was standing firm. "You fucker," he said as he opened his belt buckle, his voice cracking, no longer a man's.

I watched as he pulled it open, then unzipped his jeans, which he pushed down his legs. I jutted my chin to indicate the underpants, which he pulled down with a violent jerk. "Lift your T-shirt," I commanded.

He was every inch his father and more
so. The picture of perfection was complete. I
longed to take him in hand, suck him dry.

"Just what I thought," I said. "You'll never
be the man your father is."

I turned to go, but before I spun around
I saw the silent tears trickling down his face.
I'd succeeded in doing what I only hoped I'd
achieve later with his father: I'd broken him.

Adam, you are a man of high moral principle.
Your Project has raised several hundred
thousands of dollars to help people you
have never met to be able to live their lives
in improved health and comfort. I applaud
you, I truly do. And a part of me wishes I
could be like you, or even be you, just as you
undoubtedly have at times wished you could
be me. (Remember that party on Grant Street
the girl in our comp lit class took us to? I got
laid twice during the course of the party, once

by this chick you'd had your eye on for weeks.)
But this story I have just told you will clearly
rattle you, I know. A seventeen-year-old boy,
you ask in disgust, even though I've already
told you he was every bit a man, and, it turned
out, was running a business more effective than
his father's. But we're all good at something,
and life is one big long process of finding
that something and making it work for us. In
your case it's helping people. With someone
else it's playing the piano or writing books or
teaching. But what you are witnessing in these
pages is my own journey of discovery, first in
pulling together the disparate elements of a
mediocre business and a dysfunctional family
and improving them to the point of success,
and then—and here is where I move from mere
brilliance to genius, if you'll allow me—the
dismantling of those elements, at my discretion
and according to my plan, leaving destruction
in my wake. I had discovered my purpose and

it was to reclaim all the goodness I'd brought to that man and that family; it was mine, and I wanted it returned.

You'll agree, if you think about it long and hard enough, that such cleverness and creativity have a place in our society, just as your own talents do. In other words, I'm just as valuable to society as you are, my friend. So be careful not to judge me.

And don't forget: you never know how you'll behave in a given situation until you've been faced with it yourself.

Ziad was now working at our place every day, though Uzi never bothered to formalize the relationship, and Ziad was put through the daily humiliation of having to ask if there would be work the next day. Still, it was far better for him than the morning wait for work near the train station in Netanya, fighting to be the next from among dozens of able-bodied Arab or African men to step into some stranger's car for a day of often backbreaking work.

As I've mentioned, he was a chatterer, so I learned quite a bit about his life. The youngest son of a large brood, he'd stopped going to school after only two years, and his mother kept him home and within eyeshot from then on. When he was nineteen or so—his vagueness about numbers was appalling—his father was diagnosed with an affliction of some internal organ Ziad and I could not find in a common language, and insisted on seeing him married before he died. As always, Ziad complied, and by the time he became a father a year or two later, his own father was dead. Ziad and his young family took over his parents' home, with the mother installed on a different floor, and he and his wife continued making babies from year to year. The problem was that Ziad had no education—he told me he could barely read in Arabic; his wife was only slightly better educated, having completed elementary school—and no job training, since his parents had provided him with all his needs and kept him at home. Suddenly, in his mid-twenties, he'd had to go to work. And work didn't suit him.

I had mixed feelings about having Ziad around. On the one hand he was affable, pleasant to look at with his ruined movie-star looks, and he served as a window into a culture I knew nothing about. On the other hand, staring through that window was painful and ugly. The Palestinians were not my problem, per se—hell, I was only a new immigrant; I couldn't be held accountable for what had been done to them, what was still being done to them—but still, they were everyone's problem, and that old sixties expression about being part of the problem if you're not part of the solution always came to mind when he told me about his life.

His stories were outrageous: He had to pay a middleman to arrange the quarterly government passes that allowed him this lifeline

of working in Israel, and sometimes that fee
was so prohibitive that by the end of the month,
thanks to days of work lost to Jewish holidays
or bad weather or too much competition outside
the train station, he would have nothing left
at all. Every other week he seemed to have
some major celebration to attend—weddings,
funerals, often of people who seemed too
distant ("the father of the husband of the sister
of my wife") to merit a costly journey across
the Palestinian Authority to a remote village,
or the cash gifts he'd be expected to provide.
He wanted to buy a car, and was continually
duped by his countrymen, who tried to sell him
vehicles that would not start or would not run
more than a hundred meters or had no brakes.
There was a cousin who would hire him for
odd jobs then refuse to pay him for weeks.
Ziad would visit the man's house daily to claim
his pittance, making it a regular feature of his
trip home from work until finally the man
acquiesced. Most painful of all were the stories

of his damaged daughter, who kept the family up at nights or who would often require a trip to the emergency room or medicines they could not afford.

His stories had a Sisyphean quality to them; my limbs would grow heavy just listening. And they always had a financial twist to them; money was a constant presence, or absence. "Black," he would sometimes say. It was his shorthand way of telling me how bleak his life was. At first I was surprised that the primary object of his complaints was his fellow Palestinians, whom he called "shits" and "Muslims who did not fear God." (He himself was not religious. He did not drop to the earth in prayer five times daily as other workers did, nor did he fast during Ramadan. These two nonpractices, and a common language, were about the only things he and Ibrahim had in common.) About Jewish Israelis he was complimentary, citing compassion and largesse as typical traits, though I couldn't quite tell if this was all part of a big plan to butter me up. He was so eager and earnest that he was almost childlike. He told me often I was the only person he could talk to about his terrible life, and that much I believed.

It was beyond difficult to listen to his stories, which was the main reason I was conflicted about having him around: Who wants to listen to that? Who can stand to face that horrible reality, the check posts he passed through twice daily, the poverty, the lack of humanity and grace in his life? If I felt crushed just hearing it, for him it was obliterating. I was shocked to see how close to being nonhuman he really was. And trust me, Adam, it's not the same as you sitting at your computer raising money for people like Ziad's damaged daughter, no matter how much good you do or how good it makes you and your donors feel. Try facing one of your project people day in, day out, over coffee (or cola, his favorite, a treat when I offered it) and hearing about their blighted lives. I couldn't, not for long. Nor could I accept his regular invitations to visit his family. ("You are like a brother to me. No worry if you come into Palestine. No one kill you or hurt you.") To me, he was the front man for something too awful to witness. By listening to him I was acknowledging it and letting it seep in, but that was as much as I could do.

We had a second topic, though, beyond the tragedy of his life. Always, he would find a way to ask a question or two about Uzi and me. This clearly fascinated him, and after a while I could even sense when he was about to broach that subject by his body language, a sort of droop in his shoulders that was the embodiment of obsequiousness, as if to say, *I know I'm not allowed to ask this, but…*, and each time he seemed to find new and creative ways of asking. After a while I became amused by his efforts and started to reward him with better answers.

He was cleaning house for us every Thursday, a result of some badgering of Uzi on my part. (Ziad had sighed and said, "Women's work," but was doing it. He knew to give in quickly to everything in his life; putting up a fight or even expressing a desire never got him anywhere.) I had to keep after him to work instead of talk, and Uzi invariably had complaints about dirt under beds or hair left in a sink, but all in all I was happy to have him. Often I slipped him an extra fifty shekels from the cash Uzi left me, and Ziad, exuberant, would kiss me three times on the cheeks in the way of Palestinian men—an honor, I felt. A compliment.

Still, I wasn't prepared for what happened that particular Thursday when I entered the room we called the guest room though we never had overnight guests. He was standing stark naked by the bed, his penis half erect and his arms spread slightly to the side as if to say I have no idea how this happened and what am I supposed to do about it.

"Ziad?" I said.

He turned around so that I could see his ass, then to the front again. His body was a pleasant surprise. It's not that I hadn't thought about it—I looked at all halfway decent men, and the more spectacular-looking women, and tried to imagine them naked; I wished I could try them on like shirts on a rack, one item at a time, to see how they fit—but our relationship was so talky that I'd long since stopped wondering or fantasizing about him. And now here he was, in the buff, and mostly lovely. His skin was a soft bronze, his proportions good, he was smooth-skinned and almost hairless. Still, it was so unexpected, this mid-morning disrobing, that I wasn't quite sure what he wanted.

He motioned to me to approach in the Arab way, as if he were herding sheep. I stepped forward and he placed my hand on his cock. He was staring into my eyes. "Nice?" he asked. "Okay?"

"Sure," I said, a little breathless. He rubbed his hand on the fly of my pants and felt my hardness. "You like," he said, satisfied.

Ziad took charge at first and I let him; he had the advantage of premeditation, and for once I wasn't thinking fast on my feet. I did not worry about Uzi coming in, I did not think about the repercussions of sex with an employee, and a part of me enjoyed watching him take the lead for once, calling the shots. He motioned for me to undress and merely grunted when he saw me naked, as if I were an affirmation of what he'd envisioned. I knelt in front of him, which confused him, but he let me suck, and his pleasure was such that I wasn't quite certain he'd ever had a blowjob before.

Quickly though, he pulled my head away and moved me to the bed, where he lay down on his stomach and thrust his ass lewdly in the air, using his hands to spread his cheeks. Was this Muslim father of eight really asking me to fuck him? This was astonishing to me,

but even more so was the fact that I'd actually
forgotten what penetration was like from
this side of it. All these months with Uzi had
wiped even the memory clean. But my dick was
hard and his ass was inviting me and suddenly
I was inside him, gently, and then firmly, and
I held him tightly at the hips while I moved in
and out with increasing speed and thrust. He
made no sound. At one point I reached down
to take the pulse of his pleasure and his cock
had gone small, but I was too far gone by then
and merely pushed into him even harder until
I gave it one last good slam—just like Uzi, so
much like Uzi now—and came copiously deep
inside him.

We climbed off the bed, me dripping semen
on the floor he'd just washed, he, not hard at
all, facing me, not looking in my eyes. I was
in the afterglow, still throbbing and erect, my
cheeks flushed, a lightness in my heart. Fucking
was good, fucking was great! I'd forgotten how
great. I think I actually felt like pounding my

chest and giving a primal scream. Ziad said,
"There's a 1989 Subaru I'm saving for."

I nodded. Of course, of course. I paid him
double that day, setting a precedent without
meaning to. He did not kiss me three times on
the cheeks, but still he called me brother after
the cola, when I took him to his ride home.

Adam, Adam. The moral complexities are
multiplying, aren't they? I didn't love spending
money on sex—for Christ's sake I wasn't even
thirty and a total stud!—but after a while I
didn't see it that way at all, and anyway I gave
him double each time whether we had sex or
not. And quite often it was me servicing him
and not the other way around. I taught him
to love blowjobs. I taught him to hold back;
his experience of sex, with a single partner his
whole life whom I steadfastly refused to conjure
in my imagination, consisted of no foreplay
and as quick an orgasm as possible. He was

having a great time with me, and reported
learning to please his wife as well—who was
shocked, angry (figuring he had to have learned
this somewhere), but ultimately satiated as
she, too, learned to enjoy. (He imitated her
first-ever orgasm for me. He had followed my
instructions and the results were immediate
and thorough.) We never kissed, never held
one another except for better positioning. I did
continue to fuck him but I also let him fuck me,
which he did not badly at all. So it's like this:
he was having a good time, he was earning more
money without working harder, he was learning
new things, broadening his horizons. I ask you,
quite frankly, was this a bad thing? Sure, he was
kind of squeamish about the anal stuff, and
once I came on his face, which he didn't like,
and which produced a reaction that was as close
to anger as anything I'd ever seen from him.
But sucking me, for example: I couldn't get him
to try it even with promises not to come in his
mouth. I never insisted, not really. Not to the

point of forcing him. I let him stand his ground and he never did suck me.

Sometimes in that bed it felt—and I'm sure he felt this too—like we were, for a short time, equals. Like being naked and horizontal and horny leveled us, and that felt fair and right and good. It didn't last of course—we'd get up, clean up, dress, I'd give him money and we'd be back where we always were, where we "belonged." But still, in the long run I'm sure our relationship was good for him in every way.

In a way, between Uzi and Ziad, this whole penetration thing blew my mind. I told you that once I got started with it it felt like an addiction. I couldn't wait for the next time I would feel Uzi inside me. But it did something to me as a man, something I only started to see when the business with Ziad began. I'm not telling you anything you don't know—the physicality of it tells the whole story: one person penetrates another's body, one person inserts a piece of himself, quite intrusively, into someone else, even leaves a part of himself there as a reminder; a marking of territory, the spoils of war. And what about the other person? Well, he can be as passive as a jar being filled. It doesn't matter if he enjoys or not, or comes or not, or is in the mood or not, or accepts it or fights it. But believe me, Adam, until you've experienced it—I'm assuming here that you haven't—you don't know just how exhilarating and just how humiliating it can be. What amazed me, as a lifelong penetrator, was that I sort of "knew" this all along, but experiencing it turned out to be altogether different. I mean, women do this day in, day out. It's incredible. And like me, I'm sure some of them want it some of the time, but eventually, not much more than that.

I tried fucking Uzi back. Sometimes when I was mad at him, and sometimes when I was super horny and suddenly remembered how good fucking felt. He let me play around a little, but actual penetration? No way, that wasn't going to happen. A couple of times I brought it up with him—not in bed but at the kitchen table. (He wasn't much for talking about sex; when all was said and done he was a bit of a prude, if you can believe it.) I tried telling him that sometimes it hurt, that sometimes it was great, that I wanted him to know what it felt like and, maybe more than that, what it made me feel like. But his maleness was too ingrained, I guess, and his personality too inflexible. Once, once only, I tried forcing him. I actually tried forcing my way in. I was furious with him about something, I remember. I felt this surge inside me and I pushed; one more thrust and I would have entered him, hard. But he grabbed my arms, equally hard, and pinned me, and we panted together for a few moments, he the clear victor once again, then he jerked me off like some consolatory offering and I cried, I really cried. I suppose it was frustration. How can one army lose every time while the other takes the prize again and again? It's a war, Adam, this sex business.

An ongoing series of skirmishes with a predetermined outcome. Sure, there's adrenaline and excitement and fun and satisfaction (in war, too) but ultimately, with men and men, it's a fucking war, a war of fucking. And while once I would have said that between men and women it's not, it's something softer and more mutual, well, now I'm not so sure anymore. I'm not so sure about any of it.

And how about you, Adam? You're a gentle, straight male, unless I've somehow got you all wrong. What you do in bed with Beth— is that war? Or is some other analogy more appropriate? Fellow dancers in a ballet, perhaps, lots of lithe movements and drama and pretty arm work? Excuse me if I sound cynical or condescending, but we're being truthful here, right? In terms of masculinity quotient, if there is such a thing, I've certainly got more than you: more maleness, more testosterone, more brute sex appeal. Your boyish little body may appeal to Beth, but it's not going to get you much farther than her. But now let's factor in what each of us has done in bed with others, and I ask you: Which one of us is more of a man? Oh I know, I know, there is no equation that can answer it for us. But it doesn't stop me from thinking about it, about masculinity and maleness and what it all means. Maybe it all just comes down to those damn pheromones. Would Uzi's scent have affected you as it did me? Is all of it, everything, this whole stupid, fucking world, really just a function of desire and acting on it?

Which brings me back to Ibrahim, who, I suspected, had been just as blown away by Uzi and his damn maleness as I had. I know you've been waiting patiently or not to hear about Ibrahim, and you certainly deserve to know. But first, the children.

I didn't see Rinat for weeks and she failed to answer my text messages. I knew Nina was pretty frantic; Uzi was unmoved until one afternoon when she showed up during lunch with a small purse and large pair of shears, which she slammed onto the kitchen table and said, from between clenched teeth, "Get your keys, we're going to Tel Aviv to pick up our daughter, or I'm going to use these to cut off your balls."

"Too much drama," he muttered. But he finished his meal and followed her out the door.

They returned to Kritmonia several hours later, their first-born eighteen-year-old baby girl strapped in the backseat. She glanced up at me as she stepped from the car but said nothing. She was pale as a blank screen, her hair now a silvery blond, and cut in ragged jags she had obviously lopped off herself. Her mother had to guide her into their house, Rinat leaning all her feathery weight on Nina just to make it up three stairs.

In our own house, Uzi fell heavily onto a kitchen chair, propped his elbows on the table and pressed the balls of his hands into his eyes. His shoulders in plaid flannel were as broad as ever but they seemed to sag inward, and for a brief moment I thought he might be crying. That could have shaken my resolve, so it was fortuitous when he said, in a voice free of tears but full of exhaustion, "Jesus fucking Christ" (Israelis really say that, in Hebrew, I swear), "that girl is crazy. How did she get so crazy?" My heart hardened against him at once: your negligence, I wanted to shout, for one thing. Your inability to see her, or listen to her, or care.

The next day Nina made some phone calls, pulled some strings—though Rinat's case was so severe she needn't have bothered using connections—and Rinat was admitted to the hospital. So she was back in Tel Aviv, but in decidedly different circumstances.

I met Nina in her kitchen a few days later. Neither of us touched the spice cake I'd brought with me, and she offered no coffee. Her glorious hair was pulled back, her skin was pale, but she was resolved to help her daughter through this, and glad to have her back where she could reach her. Nina's boyfriend was nowhere to be seen, and I had a feeling she'd asked him to stay clear while she dealt with this. At one point, I admit, I had thought about messing with Nina and her new boyfriend—he seemed prey to seduction, and if not that, I could probably scare him off with invented threats from Uzi—but her happiness with him actually served my purposes with bringing Uzi down, so I left them out of my plan.

Nina told me about the apartment Rinat's lover used for shooting films. It was decked out with mirrored walls, sophisticated lighting and the latest equipment, as well as closets full of accessories and costumes. Nina hadn't been able to find the few items of clothing Rinat had taken with her. Rinat herself was confined to bed, lethargic, probably doped—the hospital was running tests. She wasn't eating or drinking and had sores on her back and between her legs that looked painful, but to which Rinat seemed oblivious. She was heavily bruised.

Through this recounting, Nina remained composed. It was the first time she was expressing what she had seen in words, and she spoke softly, precisely, and with great pain but no tears. I was impressed with her fortitude. This was a woman who had survived Uzi, and she would survive Rinat.

"We found stacks of videos, which we turned over to the police. There must be something in them they can use against the creep," she told me. He'd been at work, the accountant. They never met him.

"Uzi was pretty shaken," she said. "He was actually almost useless there. He stood around with his hands in his pockets, shaking his head."

I could picture it. For all his bulk, he could be like a huge, harmless farm animal taking up space when he wasn't in constant motion. "You know him, and you know he isn't violent," she said. "But I couldn't help wondering what he might have been capable of doing if the creep had shown up.

"I guess what I really don't understand," she continued, "or maybe really don't want to understand, is how she took this path. Oh, I know, I've read the literature and I deal with this sort of thing at work. But when you look at someone else's family the dots are easy to connect. The father that drinks or is violent. The mother who's bitter and self-absorbed, or a doormat. Crime, drugs. Incest. Really, I've seen it all. I mean, we've had a few problems, but I've still always thought of us as a fairly typical bourgeois, Ashkenazi Jewish middle-class Israeli family. So how the hell did this happen to us?"

Poor Nina. Here she was having to face her failures as a professional, a mother, even a wife. And her failures—surely she saw this as clearly as I did—were my successes. Was it not I who had proven Uzi capable of being in a relationship, I who had been making real progress with Rinat as she grew happier and fleshier in my kitchen?

Just then Ido came in through the back door. He stopped dead in his tracks and stared at us, back and forth, one to the other. "Hi honey," Nina said, holding out her hand in his direction, as if there was a chance he would walk into her arms. "We were just talking about Rinat."

That enabled him to breathe again, I could see. I turned my head so that only he could see and blew him a secret kiss. He left the room without a word. "The other kids are taking this hard," Nina said. "Orya's spending most of her time at a friend's."

And I thought: you still don't see, do you, Nina darling? You look at one for a moment, then the other slips away. You turn your attention to the second and the third one drifts off. Keep getting it wrong and you'll be left with no one, fast. Uzi Shmoozi; he's not the only reason this family is screwed up.

Yes, yes, back to Ibrahim. You recall that I had my suspicions from the first time I met him, at his father's spice shop in Acre, and those suspicions were all but confirmed with the cryptic text messages. Then Uzi had the audacity to bring Ibrahim home for a meal and I took the opportunity and began inviting him regularly. You're astonished, Adam? So was I, the first time Uzi brought him home; after that I decided it was the perfect way to study my nemesis and I participated wholeheartedly. My acting skills have proven to be stellar. I must admit, though, that while I expected to catch Uzi squeezing Ibrahim's knee under the table as he had done dangerously with me so many times, or colluding with him with a sly roll of eyes, I never did catch him, or them, at any such thing. We brought Ibrahim with us to the

cinema, to his first stage play, in Tel Aviv—
unconscionable, I thought; he had grown up
in a town famous for its fringe theater festival
as well as year-round productions but he had
never once been taken to see a play, even in
Arabic. We talked politics with him—Uzi blew
up once and nearly tossed him out when he
questioned the legitimacy of the state of Israel
and claimed Al Jazeera to be the most objective
of the region's news sources—and I urged
books on him, for those long, lonely nights in
his room. He was handsome—no, pretty is
more accurate—and soft-spoken, intelligent. If
Uzi was a lion or a bear (I changed my mind
each time I thought about this), Ibrahim was
unquestionably a fawn.

So while I hosted him and fed him and
acculturated him I was learning him. I pulled
information from him, slowly at first, but
with increasing deftness. I learned about his
married sisters and their children, whom he
adored. I learned about his wish to study

animation, thwarted, or at least postponed, by
his practical-minded father. I learned about the
close relationship he enjoyed with his paternal
grandmother, who had taught him in secret to
cook. I learned about his two older brothers
who had become deeply religious and were now
part of the Muslim Brotherhood. I learned
that he was divided between embracing Jewish
and Western values, fitting in with the elites,
and with shunning all of it and all of us. I
learned that at twenty-four he had never dated
a woman, let alone had sex with one, and was
waiting for his parents to arrange someone for
him when the time was right.

I did not write down these bits and pieces
but I stashed them away nonetheless in my
Ibrahim trove. At night, while Uzi lay lightly
snoring next to me, I lugged them into the light
of my mind and turned them over again and
again like prized trinkets.

There's more: he had beautiful hands,
which remained beautiful even with the tasks

he was assigned by Uzi. He had a charming way of waiting to speak when spoken to, never interrupting like the brash Israeli Jews around him. Even his Arabic was soft, less guttural than others'. He went home less and less often, which worried his mother. His clothes were so neat they looked pressed. He deferred to Uzi, always, as everyone did, but he challenged him, too. Spoke back to him, though invariably politely. His manners were impeccable and he was pleasant toward me, toward Uzi's family, toward customers and clients and suppliers. He was only ever less than a gentleman with Ziad. Ziad had complained to me about him several times while we were putting our clothes back on.

I watched Uzi, too; how he comported himself when Ibrahim was around. Uzi was either the best actor of us all, or not acting whatsoever. I could never quite tell.

He wasn't as rough with him as he was with others, though again that could be due to his relationship with Ibrahim's father. He made allowances for Ibrahim where heavy, dirty jobs were concerned, but these weren't really the jobs for which he had been hired.

When Ibrahim was in our home Uzi seemed indifferent. Or, more likely, doing a great job of feigning it. When I suggested bringing Ibrahim along or inviting him to dinner, Uzi wasn't always eager. I didn't know quite how to interpret that. When I asked him who had accompanied him to this or that meeting or on this or that errand, he would sometimes refrain from mentioning Ibrahim's name even when I had seen them drive off together. But what did that mean, exactly? That they were stopping en route for a tangle in some bushes, or the back of the car, or one of Uzi's favorite places up and down the coast? Or that he simply wanted to keep all worry from my head—he wasn't stupid or blind, he must have sensed my anxiety—by keeping Ibrahim squarely out of the picture? Always, always, during that period, I was in a state of unknowing that threatened to unhinge me.

Just after the Purim holiday Uzi announced that it had been raining down in the Negev desert and the conditions were ideal for truffle hunting, which meant we would be up and out before dawn the next morning. That was the first surprise: I had no idea truffles grew in Israel. The second was that Ibrahim would be accompanying us.

Israeli truffles are desert truffles and nothing like the coveted Italian and French varieties hunted with pigs, but I didn't know that yet. What I learned as we sped south—Ibrahim in the backseat, Uzi and I up front—was that they grow near a plant known picturesquely in Hebrew as a Sitting Samson, a member of the rockrose family. All we would have to do, Uzi told me, was to find those Sitting Samsons, then look for the tiny mounds of cracked earth next to them where the truffles would be hiding. What sounded simple in the car, however, was backbreaking and frustrating on the shadeless rocky desert floor. Being tall as I am, the plants and the mounds were hard for me to spot and the day was cloudless and scorching although it was still only March. Worse, I was on the alert all the time where Uzi and Ibrahim were concerned. Ibrahim, determined to succeed, asked all the right questions of Uzi about how and where to find the truffles, and in no time he'd caught on and the two of them were calling out in turn as they found another and another and yet another while I had yet to spot a single one. Uzi bellowed each time and I might have been embarrassed had we not been dozens of kilometers from other human beings. After the third or fourth he brought one over to the area in which I was prowling. He held it under my nose.

"What does it smell like?" he asked me.

The scent was so strong and so unmistakable that I thought he'd doctored it. "Semen," I said. "Yours." Though I didn't see how that could have happened I was startled nonetheless.

He roared. "Exactly!" he said. He checked
to see that Ibrahim had his back to us, then
grabbed my crotch and kissed me hard and long.
That made me feel just a little bit better, but
still I was on guard and fairly miserable.

Hours later, when they had collected a
whole bucketful and I had found only three, all
of which were so ripe they had burst through
the desert floor and were visible to the eye, Uzi
fetched equipment from the car and the three
of us built a lean-to for shade before lighting
a propane heater on which we would do some
cooking.

While Ibrahim and I were tasked with
gently removing as much sand as possible from
the truffles—removing all the sand would prove
impossible—Uzi was preparing a kind of beef
stew, the ingredients of which I had no idea he'd
brought with us.

Toward the end, when the meat was fairly
well cooked, he added our truffles and let the
stew simmer for a short while. The taste of the

desert truffles was so thin and ethereal that they almost got lost in the dish, but I praised Uzi's concoction to the heavens. Ibrahim was more guarded, but professed to like the dish well enough.

When we were cleaning up a sudden suspicion came over me and, on a hunch, I spun around to catch them in what seemed to be a sort of collusion. The long ride home was torture for me; I wanted to be away from both of them, far away. I wanted to say, Go ahead, fuck each other; I don't care. But I did care, I cared way, way, way too much and there didn't seem to be anything I could do about it.

It's fair to ask me, Adam, as I have many times myself, why I was as obsessed with all of this as I was. We were still having very good sex, and with a frequency that suited me. I was still ensconced in Uzi's home and Uzi's bed, clearly his partner or boyfriend, while Ibrahim or anyone else had the status of, I don't know—fuck-buddy, I suppose, if I were honest with myself. I myself was having somewhat pleasurable sex with Ziad, quick and perfunctory and expensive as it was, as well as the occasional hookup with someone online. (You see, Adam, I'm being brutally honest with you, to the point where I am exposing my most vulnerable and unflattering sides. That's how much I value our friendship, man.) And weren't gay men like this everywhere, always? Wasn't this part of the deal—we've balked the norm, stepped outside the traditional, the expected, and followed our true selves, or their stand-ins, our dicks. And if that was how we defined ourselves, then weren't we *asking for it* in both senses, in other words, asking for the freedom to fuck anyone, always, and asking for the consequences as well? Furthermore, I understood Uzi on some level, understood his need and his desire for more, for others. It wasn't just the biological imperative I mentioned before, but it still placed Uzi squarely in the animal kingdom, where he belonged: to wit, I fully believed, and believe today, that he was like those big predator cats (there, he is a lion once more) who won't eat prey that stands still or plays dead; prey is only of interest when in motion. So, I was the ambling antelope, the grazing gazelle, available to him whenever he desired. And that was fine, for some of the time. But what he really needed and craved was a good chase to keep him fit and alert. The hunt, the pursuit, the leap to pin the prey, to pounce on its flesh and sinews. The fresh, fresh meat, better than anything lying around at home. I got all that, I really got it. Uzi was my wild animal and one thing I loved about him was his wildness, his animalism; when he chewed a steak bone or a lamb chop, his blond-bearded jaw gnawing away, his eyes closed in exquisite pleasure, or when he plunged himself into me and hammered away, he was in his most leonine state, a true king of jungle and man. But the beast had gotten greedy—too much flesh, too much meat, too much pleasure for himself and too little for others—and I had begun to tire of this analogy, this way of his being in the world, this man. There were days when I longed to run to Nina and say, I get it now, I truly do. The satisfaction from that, however, would have been all hers, not mine. And I needed to preserve my cover, so I complained only to myself and kept my watchfulness and my energy and my creativity focused on my grand plan. I contented myself with the conundrum I puzzled over whenever I thought about Uzi, which I touched upon earlier to you, Adam: How was it, I wondered, that the things I adored about him one day were the very things I loathed the next? His earthiness, for example. I loved the fact that he was down to earth, never talked or dealt in bullshit. But it was nearly impossible to talk to him about anything spiritual or metaphysical or just plain emotional. He was thick-skinned when it came to insults but thick-skinned too when he needed to empathize with others. His lack of pettiness was refreshing but the flip side was a basic disinterest in his fellow humans. He was reliable to a fault, always who he was in every situation, but that made him unadaptable in situations that could have used some flexibility. He was male to a fault, and he was male to a fault. (Ask Beth what that means.)

But you, Adam, reasonable man that you are, you're saying, What's the big deal? So what if Uzi fooled around, especially since I did, too. (Not that this is something you'd condone in yourself, or anyone you could ever be in a relationship with; you are magnanimous with liberal attitudes where *others* are concerned.) But can you, mild unflappable man that you are, can you even begin to imagine the fire of jealousy that consumes some of us? Can you ever picture yourself, in any situation—finding Beth in bed with someone else, for example—losing all reason, experiencing with brutal physicality the same torture your soul is enduring? Hard-heart strokes, burning blood, lack of air in the lungs, all bodily systems backing up like clogged sewage and overspilling; these are uncontrollable, the physical manifestation of spiritual pain so deep that it cannot be contained or reasoned with. Oh I've read *Stranger in a Strange Land* and I know all about this lovely term—*compersion*—coined by some 1970s polyamorous commune that means "the joy one feels when one's lover is enjoying another relationship." But humans are not built that way, at least the vast, vast majority of us, and I'd go so far as to say that jealousy actually goes hand in hand with the ability to love outrageously and to make love boundlessly—truly a bright, exploding orgasm has everything in common with the rage of the jealous. Without one you cannot experience the other. So this question you wish to ask me about accepting Uzi's philandering can never be asked: in light of the intense passion I have described in these pages, it can only be clear that intense jealousy, and not compersion, is passion's twin brother.

Uzi's phone failed to provide me with additional information—I suspected he was using a different apparatus, which I thought of as his fuck phone, though I never found it—and his computer yielded almost nothing, just possible traces of porn websites like the ones I visited at home. But since his days were becoming longer and more predictably stable, I was able to spend more time on plans, arrangements and snooping than ever before. We would rise together at dawn and he would disappear for hours—which on Thursdays meant Ziad and I could do our thing without worrying about him walking in on us—then typically show up at around ten o'clock for a large breakfast I staged daily. He would head out again quite quickly, no longer needing that fast mid-morning, mid-kitchen sex he used to love, preoccupied with all he had to accomplish, and stay out until late afternoon, when he blew in hungry and agitated. I usually had soup or stew waiting for him, and a nice piece of meat with a glass of wine that would satiate him and put him to sleep, which he did until early evening, when he set out again, ostensibly to make headway on the office work he hadn't gotten to all day. This last bit of the day was crucial for me; where once I wanted him home with me to cuddle and watch television or to go out for a meal or a movie, now I wanted him away, in his office or elsewhere, so that I could spy on him in the dark. Yes, that was what I would do. I had black clothes and black sneakers I put on when he left, my sleuthing clothes. I put my phone on silent and took a tiny flashlight which I would only use if I was sure no one would spot me. Some nights I brought along my Canon.

It's not particularly pleasant to follow someone around like that, and I considered for a time actually hiring someone to do it for me. But where would I get the money for that, and besides, what would I do with the information some PI could give me? I wasn't out to sue him, I was out to punish him, to win back what he'd taken from me. And for that I needed not only the physical evidence, but the emotional charge as well. I needed to despise him. And that would only happen if I caught him *in flagrante delicto.*

You'd be surprised, though, Adam, just how intriguing it can be to spy like that, once you've gotten beyond feeling foolish or humiliated about it. Sure, there were many nights when I'd be standing there in some hiding place behind a bush or halfway up a tree and I would picture myself from without and want to laugh or cry. How the hell had I gotten myself up a tree over a man? What was I doing now with my life? At those moments I would very nearly crawl back home in shame. But I was also practiced in stoking the flames of my indignation, and besides, there would be a payoff to all this if I found what I was looking for and carried through with my plan, so I persevered.

I am still ostensibly telling you about Ibrahim, but of course his story is worthless to me without Uzi's involvement. In fact, I was spying on both of them, as much as that was possible for a single human being with limited technology at his disposal. In any case, Ibrahim tended to spend a lot of time alone in his quarters—doing I knew not what—and when he emerged he would often simply sit beside Uzi in his office, and they would talk, but only rarely, like an old couple who had run out of things to say to each other decades earlier. Those long hours in the dark taught me I had reserves of patience I hadn't known about. They taught me the value of a mission carried out well, and of my own single-minded obsessions.

There was one memorable evening when the two of them, Uzi and Ibrahim, headed out together in the truck, toward the fields. I had my camera, and thought, *This is the night.* I rode my bike as fast as I could, falling and cursing and falling and cursing again. The truck wasn't parked by the buildings, though, and I couldn't find them. Then suddenly they roared past me in the dark, nearly blowing my cover. They had finished whatever it was they'd been doing and were headed home. I returned, defeated, and more full of suspicion than ever.

I used Uzi's pickup for errands—ours or his, I rarely had errands solely my own—and it was sometimes I who dropped off or picked up Ibrahim at the Netanya train station. He only went home for a day or two every other week, and always on a weekday in order to help out during the weekend rush. On one such Tuesday I was feeling horny and irritable—Uzi hadn't touched me for several days, Ziad was only truly available on Thursdays—and when we pulled up to the station with ten minutes to spare till his train, I put my hand high on his thigh, my pinky finger dangerously close to his crotch. He bent his head to look down with the full force of his incredulity or indignation, it was hard to tell which. This wasn't part of my plan, in fact it could undermine it, but like Uzi, I didn't always think with the right head. (And you,

Adam? Do you ever fall prey to the will of your little head? You probably never let it get that far and I respect that plenty, oh sure I do, man.) Truth is, I'd imagined a threesome, though in fact I might not have been able to handle such a thing well. If I'd seen Uzi panting for him, for example, I could easily have lost my cool and ruined it for good. But that morning, with a hard-on rising toward the steering wheel, I was not thinking clearly, or at all.

After a long moment, Ibrahim looked up from my hand on his leg, turned his face toward mine, and asked, "What do you want?"

I tapped my hand, squeezed. "What do I want?" I said. "Let me think."

It was a desperate stall tactic to allow me to write a script. How good I normally was at the impromptu, the quick-on-my-feet situation, but this morning, in thrall to my desires, I was hopeless. My plan, I cried to myself. What about the plan? He sighed, as if mustering patience. His patience, in my mind, was legendary. The long hours he spent waiting for instructions from Uzi, the enormous chunks of time he spent alone. I'd seen him spend two hours with indecisive clients while he stood by, never cajoling, never butting in unless asked for help or an opinion, never even stifling boredom or irritation. He was a pack animal, a mule, sturdy and blank-faced, with limitless time and zero ambition. He would outlast us all, I thought. He and his people, they didn't need to make war with us or hold peace talks. All they had to do was stand by, steadfast and silent, while we Jews ran ourselves ragged, emoting and striving and fretting about it all until we dropped at their feet.

Now it was my turn to look into his face. If there had been a glimmer of something— acknowledgment or fear or fury—I might have pursued this, might have carried on gently exploring his willingness. Maybe he was sick of the secret he was sharing with Uzi. Maybe he was the guilty type and didn't want to hurt me after I'd been so good to him. Maybe he couldn't live with the fact of his homosexuality. I might have broken him, gotten him to confess or at least talk with me. Or I might have seduced him; frankly, I really wanted to penetrate the guy, literally stick it to him. And maybe I, too, craved fresh meat?

But there was nothing in his face, nothing at all. So I backpedaled.

"What I want, Ibrahim," I said, removing my hand from his thigh and using it to reach for his right hand in order to shake it, "is to wish you a great time at home. And to invite you to come with us on Thursday night to a concert on the grass in the amphitheater in the Alexander River park. Do you like classical music? I think the program is Beethoven, Rachmaninoff. And some modern Israeli composer."

He took my hand and shook it without conviction. "I've heard of them," he said. His voice was tight, dangerously quiet, his diction impeccably neat. "Thank you for the invitation. And thank you for the ride." He stepped out of the pickup, took from the backseat the bag of laundry he'd be presenting to his mother, slammed the door a little too hard, and strode off without another word or a backward look. I wasn't at all sure whether that was a yes.

I continued sleuthing, the methods growing more sophisticated but the results always the same. I couldn't catch them at anything substantial. So I started to focus my efforts on Phase II of the plan. I paid careful attention to the structure of Uzi's days, and when I knew he'd be away for a while I went to his office and got on his computer. I opened documents, took notes, printed copies. I maintained a well-organized file that I kept hidden behind the washing machine. The women in the shop got used to me traipsing in and out and I could see no reason why they would report me to Uzi, especially as I would sit with them and listen to them bitch about him, always sympathizing, always offering a tidbit of my own and endless words of comfort and praise for their fortitude and grace.

The problem was that I was looking more for what didn't exist, at least not on paper. I also wished to document Uzi's meetings, the deals he was shaking hands over, but even that proved difficult thanks to his inability to keep an appointment calendar. He remembered to put some of his meetings on his phone reminder, and others he instructed Miriam the bookkeeper or even the person he was meeting with to alert him just hours before he was due there. So the paper trail was short and inconclusive. At other times, when the shop and the fields and the house and the garden were truly deserted, I set about searching for his cash stashes, and in this department I was more successful. I already knew where several were and found several others without difficulty, though I did not remove any money from them; this was all just a rehearsal before the actual show. What's more, I had access to his main bank account, and although he was often overdrawn, he would sometimes move large sums of money from place to place, or make a big deposit that would soon be withdrawn, and I paid daily attention to what was happening there and could act swiftly if need be.

I'll admit that my methods grew a little desperate at this stage; it wasn't easy to spend so much time looking and so little time finding, all the while keeping up appearances at home. Sometimes I thought Uzi might be on to me—he'd give me slow, sidelong glances while chewing, or stop in the middle of the room just to gaze at me (that used to mean he was about to pull me to him for sex, but not so much anymore)—and I would redouble my efforts at normalcy, with elaborate meals, a back rub, special attentiveness to his retelling of his day, sex in the shower, while redoubling my sleuthing efforts, too.

Battling an invisible enemy and maintaining good relations with the visible ones can be taxing to the point of madness. There were days when I fell into bed midday with a headache and from sheer exhaustion, my resolve waning and my energy low. But invariably, someone or something would trip a wire: Uzi's phone might ring at dinner and after looking at the caller's name he would return the phone to his pocket, unanswered; or Ibrahim might appear from around a building, then Uzi, too, only twenty seconds later; or a mysterious car might zoom down our quiet street late at night, Uzi sauntering into the house moments later; or after three days of no sex he might make love to me but fail to come, a clear sign he'd been spending his seed elsewhere and in great quantities. These signs and others were all I needed to renew my vigor and conviction, and off I'd go again with pen and paper and camera, with binoculars (no need to purchase, I found them, slightly cracked and very dirty, in a box in the spice shop), with a flashlight, with my silenced phone that never rang anyway.

But weeks and weeks of this took their toll. And still they evaded me, those two clever lovers. By now Uzi would have taught Ibrahim everything he knew about sex and exactly how he liked it. By now they would be lovers, not just fuck-buddies. I couldn't look at Ibrahim's lips without imagining them pursing to pincer Uzi's nipples the way he liked for the purpose of bringing him deep pain and pleasure, or hovering like a butterfly over Uzi's neck, his furred belly, his calloused work hands; or worst of all, pressed against Uzi's mouth in a passionate kiss. Ibrahim would be in love with him by now, envisioning himself in Uzi's house and Uzi's bed after I'd been deposed. I had to turn away at those moments, unable to stomach Ibrahim's feigned innocence, the doe eyes, the lips that pretended not to know the pinnacles of physical and emotional ecstasy I knew they were experiencing. My life was becoming torture and the need to implement the final stages of my plan was growing, and fast.

And then it hit me, so hard that I stumbled off the path I was walking down to the beach for the exact purpose of thinking about all this: I didn't have to catch them at anything! After all, Adam, in real life we rarely get closure on the things that bother us most: We don't catch the lovers in bed. We don't find the incriminating email. We don't know why that lover or friend suddenly stopped speaking to us. We merely have our suspicions, and go crazy from them.

They had been outsmarting me for so long that now it was my turn to outsmart them. I ran back to the house to prepare a new list, something far more clever. You'll say devious, but when dealing with the underhanded, the cheat, the liar, one can scarcely afford not to think like him. And what a relief to know I would no longer have to climb my spying trees or hide in bushes or even don my black sleuthing clothes. All that was behind me now! The real work, I saw now, would be in my imagination.

For the next few days I worked in a feverish flurry of activity, very nearly giving myself away to Uzi when I lost track of time and sat too long at the computer, failing to start dinner or hear him tramp onto the porch. I understood now that one photo was all I needed, one single photo to hammer home what a letter full of words would do with far less punch, and since I had no such photo in my possession thanks to Uzi's and Ibrahim's noteworthy caution, I would have to conjure one on my own. Of a series of photos I'd shot on our truffle-hunting expedition, Uzi and Ibrahim both by mid-morning shirtless in the springtime desert sunshine, there was one, I recalled, one photo I'd snapped from a distance with a telescopic lens, of the two of them in apparent collusion, too close for my taste, Uzi touching Ibrahim on the chest or upper arm. It had rankled me, that image, both when I snapped it and when I developed it. Surely with some cropping and some manipulation I would be able to include it in the envelope.

The synapses were sparking; I was on fire with creativity. I only wish I could show you the full results of my work, the depth of cleverness and talent necessary for such an operation. But those results are in other hands now.

A full week passed between the time I had my epiphany and the completion of my project, seven days of intensive labor to assemble all the necessary documents. For good measure I wiped everything clean of fingerprints, though that was surely unnecessary and a little paranoid of me. I gathered all my materials into four large manila envelopes and hid them in the lining of my suitcase, a place where no one would ever find them.

I was a mere days away from completing my work and sat with a calendar to begin the countdown. (I know you're riveted to the couch, Adam, I feel your butt boring into these very cushions I'm sitting on. You are unable to move, unable to fill the water glass you drank to the bottom an hour ago, unable to sprint to the bathroom for a pee.) I worked with the train schedule, ordered an airline ticket, gave explicit instructions to the taxi company. Everything was in motion now, there was no room for error. In the meantime, to maintain an aura of normalcy, I laundered, I cooked. I edited a new brochure for the spice shop. I answered email questions from a local journalist.

Then it was Wednesday, at last. In the very late afternoon, when the sun had set but light still glimmered slantwise over the horizon, and Uzi was napping after a hard day battling the elements, I started my work. Wearing my sleuthing clothes for the last time—I would be leaving these behind as well, I'd decided—I moved about in the sheds, the greenhouses and the garden quietly, with purpose, the map I'd made serving as my invaluable guide and the great expediter; in fact, the whole operation took me only about forty minutes. I carried with me a black bag, into which I stuffed everything without looking at what I was finding, and was careful to replace soil to the ground or rusty teapots to their high shelves or *Guide to Spices of the Middle East* to the pile of books behind Uzi's desk—whatever the retaining receptacle, I made sure it was back in its place looking undisturbed and untouched.

When Uzi awoke I made him coffee with cream and a little more sugar than I normally spooned in, and sliced him a piece of the banana bread with turmeric, fenugreek and clove that I'd baked earlier in the day. I sat next to him at the edge of the bed as he nibbled and sipped; at one point, just as I was gazing toward the window and the view I'd grown accustomed to but would be seeing no longer, he cupped his hand around my neck and stroked the side of my head with his large, rough thumb. I looked toward him and he was gazing into my eyes, a small smile nearly hidden under his beard and mustache. I felt everything move inside me all at once: a release of the sphincter, a plunge of the belly, an engorgement of the heart. My vertebrae unknitted, my face muscles slackened. His touch and his gaze, which carried both the strength and the gentleness of wind and water to move me, spoke of love. There was no denying it. You see, Adam? I could have made him out to be a monster, but I've been truthful and objective, and here I am showing you that beautiful moment when he had love written all over him and it was pouring out of his eyes and his hand into me. And I thought about what I was about to set in motion and a part of me sobbed inside. Why did this have to happen? Why couldn't we have continued as we were—lovers, business partners, friends? A family even. I could have remained here, made my mark with him and through him. We could have renovated a little, found ourselves a nice community of friends. Traveled, as the business brought more ease. Maybe I could have talked him into having a baby, if I decided I really wanted to go that route. I could have pursued other interests, too. Reading. Photography. We could have joined a local group of cyclists for weekend outings. We could have grown old together. I am not even thirty but I could picture it, the two of us walking the lovely lanes of our village, making our way slowly down to the sandy beach, beautiful and dramatic in every season and every type of weather. All this I pictured at the edge of our bed, in that window of a moment when he set down the banana bread on the plate and the coffee mug next to it and had only me in his heart and in his mind, in his body and in his soul.

His phone rang, and though he ignored it I felt certain it was Ibrahim, impatient, calling to find out when Uzi would return to the office, the greenhouses. The guy was getting more and more brazen, phoning at any hour. I composed myself, returned Uzi's dishes to the kitchen, hovered about him while he threw on his clothes. By the time he stalked out the door I was back in control and ready to continue.

At my desk, the window blinds shut behind me, I removed the contents of my black bag and sorted through it, pulling cash from plastic bags, crumpled envelopes, sheets of folded paper and, in one case, the core of a roll of toilet paper. I threw the containers away, counted the hoard—it was far larger than I'd imagined—and separated it into two unequal piles, then placed the larger pile in one legal-size envelope and fastened the smaller to my passport and other important documents with a rubber band. That operation over, I moved to my computer. The bank loan Uzi had requested had been deposited into his private account two days earlier; it was still there, and he was two hundred thousand shekels in the black. I logged out and shut down the computer.

That night I made love to Uzi for the last time. It was not, certainly, our best ever, but more like an amalgam of all our many months of lovemaking: rough and gentle, fast and slow, selfish and selfless. I gave myself to him almost wholly, but held back the part of me that had been so affected earlier that evening. It was fine. I carried his semen in me and fell asleep that way; I was happy to keep that much of him inside me till morning, almost sorry that as always it would swim and swim but find nothing at all to fertilize.

Ziad, unaware that this would be his final cleaning session in our house, arrived on time at seven that Thursday morning. We hadn't had sex for several Thursdays, ever since I'd asked him point blank about his enjoyment and his answers, each time I rephrased the question, came back to the issue of money. It hit me hard to think that although his cock had been erect and his ass pliant and open to most anything I wanted, he saw this solely as a business transaction, a way to alleviate the unbearable burden of his life. There was nothing gay about him, or bisexual. And when he came, I forced myself to realize, he did so with pain and remorse. He never gazed at me with longing the way Uzi did, or more accurately the gazes and the longing were for cash and a tiny bit of ease. Once this was clear to me, I could no longer invite him to bed. So you see, Adam, that my moral compass isn't all that different from yours in the end.

I was busy that day, in and out of the house, so that we didn't even have time for coffee or food together. When he finished, at three, I handed him his envelope, the fat one I'd prepared the previous evening.

"Ziad, this is money given to me by a rich uncle in America. He wanted me to find someone who really, really needs it."

Ziad glanced at the envelope I was holding. He could see it was stuffed full, bursting. He looked into my eyes and I could see the fear there, and confusion. He shook his head three times quickly in the way Arabs do as a way of wordlessly asking the meaning of this. But I saw in that gesture another set of questions: Was this a trick of some sort? Will I get in trouble for accepting? Will the police stop me and accuse me of theft not five minutes from here?

"It's for you, Ziad, take it," I said, pushing it into his hands.

Still it was hard for him. He barely grasped the envelope and I feared its contents would spill to the floor.

I smiled. "Don't look so unhappy! Good things happen sometimes. Nice surprises."

As I said this I realized how untrue that was. For Ziad, there were only bad things. Nasty surprises. This windfall was so unimaginable to him, so undreamable, that he looked fairly miserable.

His hands were trembling. He pulled me close for a three-cheek series of kisses. "You are closer to me than my brother," he said softly.

"Listen, Ziad," I said, grasping his shoulders and staring straight into his eyes. "You have to understand something. There is a lot of money in that envelope. It's about as much money as you earn in a year. It will buy you that Subaru you want."

"Subaru," he repeated. A mantra.

"And more. But you must be careful. Do not tell anyone about this money. Not Jews, not Arabs. If you can help it, don't tell your wife, either. Can you keep it a secret?"

"A secret." He was dazed. I don't think he was really hearing me. I shook him a little.

"Ziad, this is important. Don't get all weird on me now. Are you listening?"

"Listening," he said.

There were more kisses, more words of thanks and praise, a flow of tears before I could get him out of my kitchen and on his way home. And suddenly I knew that this money would be a disaster for him, that somehow a man with his rotten life, his horrible luck, would never manage to derive any good from such a windfall. He would slip and tell a cousin, and thieves would slit his throat. He would count it in public and it would be taken from him in moments. He would lose it, he would get stopped at the border crossing and accused of a crime, he would squander it, he would waste it, he would get caught in a windstorm that would carry the bills high in the air where they would blow to the Jews, not the Palestinians, settling in people's manicured gardens and beside their swimming pools, plucked from the green grass by happy children. How could any good come from something so completely outside Ziad's experience of misery and deprivation? And worse, it would be the watershed of his life, the great missed opportunity. It would be what finally pushed him from a vague unhappiness with his life to a hardened bitterness that would dog him to his death. I thought all this as I watched his new worry burden him, his lope awkward as he pressed one palm against his thigh where the money bulged thickly in his pocket. There would be no salvation here. Not where the problems were intractable and the future hopeless.

But Ziad was no longer my problem. I had done what I could, and now I had my own concerns to which to return. It was already a quarter past three and I had an hour to throw my belongings into my suitcase before I had to get to the train station. Packing was easy, though, as I had already sorted through what I would take and what I would leave behind. When the case was ready I shoved it under the bed. I put three of the four manila envelopes into my backpack, along with the envelope of documents I had stashed behind the washing machine that was now addressed to a man I'd spoken to in the Income Tax Authority. A smaller, thinner envelope was addressed to a Ms. Esther Sapir in the Plant Protection and Inspection Services Department of the Ministry of Agriculture that included purchase invoices for the large quantities of the malathion, acetamiprid, cypermethrin and dimethoate pesticides that Uzi was using on his "organic" herbs and spices. The Interior Ministry envelope provided charts of cash transactions concluded between Uzi and many of his suppliers and customers with no other documentation, like receipts. I walked to the entrance of our village, where I knew I could flag down an exiting car that would get me to the Netanya train station in mere minutes.

I boarded the 4:47 p.m. northbound train and disembarked at Acre, where the weather was a tad cooler, after a comfortable hour-and-a-quarter journey. I had time to walk, which I knew would clear my head and would allow me to stop by a post office in the new part of town before reaching the walls of the Old City. I mailed the Income Tax Authority and Agriculture Ministry envelopes, and ten minutes later was already entering the narrow stone warrens of the Old City. Once inside I had no trouble locating three young locals who would serve as my emissaries. To each I gave a fifty-shekel note drawn from Uzi's cash stashes, and handed

him a manila envelope. One bore the name
of Ibrahim's father, Muhammad Akkawi; the
other two were addressed to Ibrahim's brothers,
Nabil and Abdullah, about whom I'd exhumed
so much information from Ibrahim, especially
their extreme devotion to Islam. I was sorry
not to meet them or be able to hand them the
envelopes myself. I was sorry not to experience
their reactions when they opened the packets to
find an explicit, accusatory, revealing letter from
me (anonymous, of course) and the photograph
I had included of their sweet young brother and
son looking very much like big Uzi's darling
playtoy. I smiled thinking of the perfection of my
work. There was always the chance they would
confront Ibrahim, or even Uzi, but with these
types, I knew from Nina, they acted hotly, rashly;
there would be little talk and lots of action.

Incidentally, I wore a hood and sunglasses
for this part of the operation. Only Muhammad
had ever seen me, but still I wanted to preserve
my anonymity as much as possible, for obvious

reasons. And I had prepared three different envelopes to be hand-delivered by three different boys so that even if one messed up, the message and the photos would surely hit their mark nonetheless. There was no way that all three could fail to arrive in the hands of the Akkawi family, and for that matter, even if they did not, whoever did find them in the whole of the Old City of Acre, where everyone knows everyone, would recognize Ibrahim and make sure his family was involved. My plan was certainly foolproof.

I snagged a falafel sandwich—we never got anything quite this fresh and delicious in our part of the country—grabbed a taxi and returned to the train station in time to catch the 7:22 back to Netanya. On the way I took out my laptop and, as according to my grand plan and merely by entering a few codes and answering a few questions using Uzi's bank-approved mechanism for moving large sums from account to account, I was able to transfer three-quarters of the funds there to an international account I'd opened the week before and could access with my new bank card anywhere in the world, with the ability to withdraw funds in any currency. It was a sum I felt comfortable taking when I calculated the work I'd put in and the money I'd helped earn him and which he would continue to earn in my absence, thanks to all my excellent innovations. At Netanya, a taxi awaited me as planned, and it got me back to Kritmonia just before nine o'clock, precisely on schedule. I instructed the driver to pop his trunk open and leave it that way, and to keep his engine running. I passed him a hundred-shekel note to ensure he wouldn't take off on me and I headed into the house I had lived in for nearly a year and was about to abandon.

As always, I could sense whether Uzi was in the house or not, and indeed he was, so before I pursued him at the back of the house I pulled my hidden suitcase out to the porch and dropped my backpack next to it. I found him lying on our bed in a pair of plaid boxer shorts. He was watching one of those National Geographic shows he loved, with men battling the elements or men battling machines or men battling other men. He often talked to the television, giving instructions to this guy or that and labeling them "idiot" or "crazy" when they didn't follow his advice and only made their problems larger.

I took up the controls and turned off the set. I was slightly nervous, but I wasn't about to let the normalness of this evening or Uzi's broad and hairy chest get the better of me, and the rightness of what I was doing emboldened me.

He looked up at me, expectant more than annoyed that he would never know whether those men in Alaska would catch the big fish.

"I'm leaving," I said.

"When will you be back?" he said.

"I'm not coming back," I said.

"Until when? And where are you going?"

"I'm leaving you," I said. I didn't want to provide details about where I was heading the moment I left this house.

He pulled himself upright into a sitting position. Now I had his attention. "What do you mean?" he asked, frowning.

"I mean that it's over, Uzi." My voice grew softer when I said this. I needed to stoke my anger. "I mean that I'm sick of your entitlement."

"Entitlement?" he asked. Even though I was speaking in Hebrew the word confused him.

"Yeah. Like you feel that you deserve everything."

"Who said I feel like I deserve everything?" he asked.

"You. All the time."

"Like what?" he asked. "Give me some examples."

This was exasperating. I hadn't gotten to say what I'd rehearsed, and we weren't even dealing with my departure. I thought about the taxi and wondered how long he'd wait before driving off with my hundred shekels and no way for me to leave.

"You want examples? Okay, I'll give you examples." I stood there, glaring at him, while his face looked unmoved. And then the strangest thing happened: I couldn't think of anything. My mind blanked on the hundred things large and small that drove me insane about Uzi's selfishness. In fact, only one burned brightly before my eyes, the one I wished to save for last, but there was no time for the script now, so I plunged right into it.

"Men," I said. "Guys. You've got lots of them, I know. And you chat with them and you email them and you talk to them. And of course you meet them. Sex and sex and more sex. How do you think that makes me feel?"

"What? What are you saying?" he asked. So he wasn't denying anything.

"What am I saying?" He was handing me back my rightful fury, and it felt good. "I'm saying that you're cheating."

"Cheating you?"

"Of course!"

"But you're here in my bed, my house. We have great sex. We love each other. How is that cheating?"

I took in a sharp breath. Had he said love? We love each other? Why was he only uttering this word for the first time tonight?

"It's cheating because it's not something we agreed on or even discussed," I said. "I've been watching you, Uzi. I know what you've been up to."

"What I've been up to?"

"You know what I'm talking about."

"Here and there a little porn. Why do you care so much? Everyone does it."

How good even the slightest confirmation felt, at last!

"And anyway," he added, "you've never talked to me about what you get up to on Thursdays with Ziad."

I must admit, I was dumbfounded. "What do you mean?" I asked, unconvincingly I'm sure.

"I figured out you must be having sex. Lots of little clues. Is that part of the agreement you were talking about?"

"There was no agreement, Uzi, spoken or unspoken. And I don't know what you're talking about where Ziad is concerned."

"Why is that fair?" he asked quietly. "You can have sex with Ziad but I must not even think about other men?"

"I never said anything about sex with Ziad!" I shouted. Now Adam, you of course know that there had been, at one time, something minor and insignificant between Ziad and me. But you also know that this was the result of my frustration at what was happening with Uzi. It was my counterbalance. It kept me from breaking dishes or taking a knife to Uzi's balls or setting the house on fire. Uzi should thank God I'd had Ziad!

"I don't like the way this conversation is going," I said. "And we haven't even discussed Ibrahim."

"What about Ibrahim?" Uzi asked. The great actor. The look of incomprehension on his face was flawless.

"That you've been fucking him since the day you brought him here."

Uzi jumped from the bed and for a brief second I thought he was going to hit me. "Are you crazy?!" he asked. "Where did you come up with that idea?"

"Don't even try to get out of this, Uzi," I said, furious now. "You've been lusting after his sweet ass from the time we both met him in his father's office. I'm so sick of him, sick of the two of you—"

"What, the two of us? There is no two of us!" He was shouting now, too.

"You've been sneaking around here, since ... the beginning with him. And I can't take it anymore."

"You know something, you're crazy," he said. "It's all in your head, all this fucking. Men on the Internet. Ibrahim. What about my

Thai workers? Am I fucking them, too? Kiti, Sonakon? Am I fucking them?"

He was standing across from me, his bald head flushed red, his thick arms spread wide, his belly pulled tight in anger. I could see his dick pressing at his shorts and I averted my eyes.

"It's too late for this, Uzi. Just too late."

"You want to leave?" he said. "Fine, then leave. But don't blame me for that. If anything, your behavior is worse than mine. But who cares? I can live with that. After all, no two members of a couple are ever exactly equal in the way they love each other."

We stood facing one another, just breathing. I knew that if I stepped up to him now and buried my head in his neck, all would be forgiven by morning. I haven't mentioned that to you about him, but although he was quick-tempered, nothing of it ever remained. He bore no grudges, ever.

It was tempting, I want to tell you. I knew, I had always known, that I would miss the really good times I had had with him. I would miss what we had built together. Mostly, perhaps, I would miss the comfort and excitement of his body, and the feeling he gave me when he made love to me, when I still loved him.

The only thing I could do was return to the script, tattered though it was. "I've given you so much," I said, softer now. "I helped repair your business. I helped repair your family."

"That's right," he said. "And I've given to you in return. That is what couples do."

I couldn't take anymore. It was lies he was telling, or half-truths. I didn't know. And I would never know. I would never really and truly know, and that was impossible for me. I couldn't live this way, never knowing, always caring. If I stayed, if I undid all I had done, would I feel any different tomorrow or the next day? Would I trust him? Should I trust him? This lack of clarity would be my undoing, I knew it. Maybe he wasn't evil, maybe I even understood some of his entitlement. But nothing would ever change, not with him. I'd forever be wondering about Ibrahim, about potential other Ibrahims, about whom he was giving his seed to, seed that was mine by rights.

Jake from grad school had had the same problem, it's what unraveled him. With me, he'd been able to figure out who he really was—sexually, artistically, you name it. But then he got possessive. He wanted too much of me. The day before he killed himself I caught him following me. I was with this guy and he was outside the door the whole time, sobbing. It was a mess. But I never thought he'd do anything so stupid. Jake had everything going for him and then he blew it on a relationship he mistook for love. He was there with me and Uzi in that room, I'm telling you, Adam, Jake was right there next to me. He'd been dogging me since his death, from before his death, he'd hounded me right out of grad school by jumping from that window but I'd managed to keep him at bay pretty much the whole time I was in Israel. Then suddenly he was there, and I knew I wasn't willing to wind up like that, like somebody's prisoner, or a prisoner to my own desires and obsessions.

"I have to go," I told Uzi. I did not move.

He sat down on the bed facing the television and tapped the controls. On the screen, men were arguing while a blizzard engulfed a frozen lake.

I turned to go, walked down the hall without glancing into the rooms, and gathered my bags. Nina was on her porch, with her boyfriend and Ido and Orya. I did not look in their direction and none of them said a word as I headed to the idling taxi. I slammed the trunk closed and sped away.

Uzi would find his copy of the packet of photos stuffed into the cereal box he would open in the morning, when I was gone. He would discover the missing money in the days and weeks to come. Money, I remind you, that I was owed. I still feel good about how much I gave to Ziad, no matter what became of him or the money.

Landing in New York, my plan finished and done, I had nowhere to go. Until I looked up at the departures board and saw a flight to this town listed. Instead of flying, however, I made my way to the Greyhound station and in a not unreasonable number of hours found myself on this very sofa with a cup of tea in my hands.

Adam, I have provided you with a wealth of information designed to prove to you the veracity of my story, though by now I'm sure you see it needs no verification: it is true. However, if you are tempted, as a man of lofty principles, to right the wrongs you perceive have been committed in these pages, let me tell you that most identifying features have been changed. Uzi is not Uzi, Nina is not Nina, Kritmonia is obviously not Kritmonia, thus the Kritmonia Herb and Spice Company surely does not exist. (I'm particularly proud of *Kritmonia*; although it's a bit odd in Hebrew it would make a far better name than the dull Zionistic moniker that the village actually bears.) Ibrahim and his family are not who I've led you to believe. Hapless Ziad, who is not Ziad, may or may not have eight children, one of them damaged, or not. Oh, I know, I promised you the truth throughout, and in fact I have delivered it. But where the truth would hurt me or others I refrained, restrained myself, and in time Uzi became Uzi even in my mind as he should in yours, Ibrahim became Ibrahim, and so on. The truth is a wily creature, Adam. If you haven't learned that yet, you should now, if only to ensure your survival. And the survival of your relationship with Beth, if that is still of relevance.

Truth is protean, it changes from person to person, it changes within a person, and yet remains the truth. The truth, in this case, is in the emotions and experiences of the characters I have drawn for you in words and pictures, if not in their names or their identifying features.

Think of the truth as a deep well, and each bucketful of cool water that emerges as one gulp of it. Your thirst should be quenched by now.

Your name, in its true form, appears throughout this document, though for that matter it is as generic as they come: Did you know that in Hebrew *Adam* simply means "man"? You, my friend, could be the stand-in for all men everywhere. The average man, the standard man, any man, the man for all times and places.

My name, on the other hand, appears nowhere here, for reasons now obvious to you after reading this letter. At one point, perhaps, I thought part of my motivation in writing to you might be the same reason young Ido (who isn't really Ido, of course) took pride in telling me about his illicit business: What good is success if no one knows about it? But while I still take pride in my clever machinations and manipulations, I do not take particular pride in having had to carry them out in the first place. Moreover, as I've noted, closure is rare and revenge is even more rarely sated. I do not know what became of Uzi or Ziad or Rinat, I do not know what Ibrahim's family did to him, if anything, and I probably never will.

Finally, you will find an extra twenty thousand dollars in your Project account. (You think you are cautious but I watched you put in your code from about the third day I was here, and you've never changed it.) Please consider that my thanks: a parting gift. And an ablution of sorts. These four months have given me ample time to think, and I still believe I was right in acting as I did, though my margin of error and doubt is larger than I'd believed. Jealousy is a dangerous motive, and revenge its sharpest weapon. I am off to find my destiny elsewhere, a little sadder, a little wiser.

But in this last breath of time between the knowledge you have gained about me and about life, and my departure, I invite you to join me at the small hotel down the street, in the room with the balcony overlooking the park, if only for a short while. Come, Adam. You know you want to and you know you will.

Yours, quite sincerely,
XXX

ACKNOWLEDGMENTS

This book may not have been written without Adina Hoffman and Peter Cole; the National Endowment for the Arts; and Vermont Studio Center.

Lior Lev Sercarz of La Boîte and his book *The Art of Blending* taught me so much about the importance of spices. Shlomo Ravid provided valuable insider information about early moshav life in Israel. Ghiora Aharoni gave me excellent advice and a cover design that perfectly encapsulates the book.

I am grateful for excellent readers: Abby Frucht, Joan Leegant, Gay Bergman, Lucy Hungerford, James Scudamore, Lynn Holstein.

Several friends and relatives made my life easier at certain important moments during the writing of this book: Karyl Nairn, Kate and Erik Proehl, Jill Horowitz, Ruthie Almog.

From my first conversation with publisher Judith Gurewich I knew I would love Other Press, and that feeling only grew stronger with time. Enormous thanks to Judith and the entire team for their professionalism and passion.

My agents Robert Guinsler of Sterling Lord Literistic and Deborah Harris of the Deborah Harris Agency are readers, friends and advisers who stand with me always but never let me off easy.